U0085005

序　言

　　報考插大考試時，各校試題題型不盡相同，但字彙是必考題型。為了幫助同學精通插大字彙，我們特別蒐集歷屆各校插大試題，利用電腦做精密統計，整理出最常考的 1000 個單字，編輯成「**插大必考1000字**」一書。

　　本書按照單字詞性編排，共分成**名詞、動詞、形容詞、副詞**等四部分，方便同學記憶。同時，為了幫助讀者理解字義及記憶，書中部分單字也加注字根字首分析，如 anthropology :「研究人類的學問」即為「人類學」，如此一來，簡單易背。

anthrop + ology
|　　　　　|
man + *study*

此外,在書中,每隔六頁即附一回 **Check List**,以配合題形式,做同義字測驗,隔頁即附同義字整理,方便同學比較,並進一步提昇同學字彙能力。只要熟記本書所收錄的單字,相信同學任何單字考題,都能輕易掌握,此外,本書也適用於準備參加「**中高級英語檢定測驗**」,以及「**TOEIC 測驗**」的讀者。

這本書能夠順利完成,要特別感謝外籍老師 Laura E. Stewart 的仔細校對,黃淑貞小姐負責內文版面編排,白雪嬌小姐設計封面。

全書雖經仔細編審校對,但仍恐有疏漏之處,望請讀者不吝批評指正。

編者 謹識

名 詞

accommodation (ə,kamə'deʃən)

n. 住宿

The *accommodations* at this hotel are not only adequate but also inexpensive. (80 淡江)

accomplishment (ə'kamplıʃmənt)

n. 成就

One of her greatest *accomplishments* was winning a gold medal at the 2000 Olympics.

(89 成大,86 逢甲)

acquaintance (ə'kwentəns) *n.* 認識的人

I don't know him very well; he is only an *acquaintance* of mine. (81 台大,80 淡江)

adolescent 〔͵ædḷ'ɛsn̩t 〕 *n.* 青少年

Adolescents in Taiwan are under a lot of
pressure. (85 逢甲)

advantage 〔 əd'væntɪdʒ 〕 *n.* 優點

A good command of English is a great
advantage when you apply for a job.

(88 銘傳，81 台大)

adversity 〔 əd'vɜsətɪ 〕 *n.* 逆境

Many can bear *adversity*, but few contempt.

(83 文化)

ad	+	vers	+	ity
|		|		|
to	+	*turn*	+	*n.*

advertisement 〔͵ædvɚ'taɪzmənt 〕
n. 廣告

They put an *advertisement* in the magazine
to promote their new product. (85 文化)

affection 〔 ə'fɛkʃən 〕 *n.* 感情

There is nothing stronger than a mother's *affection* for her children.

(90 輔大，87 中原，80 淡江)

agency 〔'edʒənsɪ 〕 *n.* 代辦處

Employment *agencies* help workers to get jobs, and find workers for people who need them. (84 中興)

agent 〔'edʒənt 〕 *n.* 代理人

Mr. White is my *agent*; he can make decisions for me. (82 台大)

agony 〔'ægənɪ 〕 *n.* 痛苦

In his final *agony* he called for religious comfort. (82 中興)

alliance 〔 ə'laɪəns 〕 *n.* 聯盟

These two airlines will create an *alliance* in the near future.

（87 台北大，86 中興）

al +	li	+ ance
|	|	|
to +	*bind* (綁) +	*n.*

allowance 〔 ə'lauəns 〕 *n.* 零用錢

Peter's parents give him a monthly *allowance* of 5000 dollars. （88 政大）

alternative 〔 ɔl't𝟥nətɪv 〕 *n.* 替代品

Scientists are looking for *alternatives* to replace some of the more expensive metals.

（89 輔大，86 銘傳，82 交大）

alter +	native
|	|
other +	*n.*

amendment 〔 ə'mɛndmənt 〕 *n.* 修正

The National Assembly has made several *amendments* to the R.O.C. constitution.

（86 銘傳）

amusement 〔ə'mjuzmənt〕 *n.* 娛樂

The community center provides townspeople with various kinds of *amusement*.

（88 銘傳，80 淡江）

ancestor 〔'ænsɛstɚ〕 *n.* 祖先

Our *ancestors* came from Fukien Province in mainland China.

（83 淡江）

an	+ ces	+ tor
before	+ go	+ 人

angle 〔'æŋgḷ〕 *n.* 角度

Looking at the painting from this *angle*, we can see a hidden image. （86 台大）

anthropology 〔,ænθrə'pɑlədʒɪ〕

n. 人類學

He was interested in *anthropology*. （86 私醫）

anthrop	+ ology
man	+ study

appetite 〔'æpə‚taɪt 〕 *n.* 食慾

Mother doesn't feel well now and has lost her *appetite*. (86 逢甲)

applause 〔 ə'plɔz 〕 *n.* 鼓掌

After the performance, the pianist received a great round of *applause*. (89 成大，81 清大)

appreciation 〔 ə‚priʃɪ'eʃən 〕 *n.* 感激

I wrote a thank-you letter to her in *appreciation* of her help. (88 中央)

```
ap + preci + at(e) + ion
 |      |       |      |
to +  price  +  v.  +  n.
```

approach 〔 ə'protʃ 〕 *n.* 方法

When learning a foreign language, the best *approach* is the study of the spoken language. (86 銘傳)

•Check List•

( ) 1. accommodation   A. anguish

( ) 2. accomplishment   B. revision

( ) 3. adolescent   C. cooperation

( ) 4. advantage   D. forefather

( ) 5. adversity   E. lodging

( ) 6. affection   F. benefit

( ) 7. agony   G. emotion

( ) 8. alliance   H. achievement

( ) 9. alternative   I. handclapping

( ) 10. amendment   J. substitute

( ) 11. amusement   K. gratefulness

( ) 12. ancestor   L. recreation

( ) 13. applause   M. teenager

( ) 14. appreciation   N. method

( ) 15. approach   O. hardship

Vocabulary Ratings

5–7 *Good*   8–11 *Very Good*   12–15 *Excellent*

·Synonyms·

1. accommodation
   = lodging

2. accomplishment
   = achievement

3. adolescent
   = teenager

4. applause
   = handclapping

5. appreciation
   = gratefulness

6. amusement
   = recreation
   = entertainment

7. approach
   = method

8. alliance
   = cooperation

9. alternative
   = substitute

10. amendment
    = revision
    = alteration

11. affection
    = emotion
    = love

12. ancestor
    = forefather

13. advantage
    = benefit

14. agony
    = anguish
    = pain

15. adversity
    = hardship
    = difficulty

approval〔ə'pruvḷ〕n. 贊成

Does our proposal meet with the boss's
approval? (88中正)

aptitude〔'æptə,tjud〕n. 性向

The students take an *aptitude* test to
determine what their talents are. (86逢甲)

apt + itude
| |
fit + *n.*

aqua + rium
| |
water + *place*

aquarium〔ə'kwɛrɪəm〕n. 水族館

In an *aquarium*, we can see a wide variety
of fish and aquatic animals. (86私醫)

aroma〔ə'romə〕n. 芳香

The *aroma* of coffee makes me feel cheerful
and comfortable. (86清大)

assumption 〔 ə'sʌmpʃən 〕 n. 假設

The scientist made an *assumption* that there was no life in the lake. (85 淡江)

atheist 〔 'eθɪɪst 〕 n. 無神論者

An *atheist* does not believe in God or any gods. (82 淡江)

a	+ the	+ ist
without	+ *god*	+ 人

audi	+ torium
hear	+ *place*

auditorium 〔 ˌɔdə'torɪəm 〕 n. 演講廳

Professor Thompson's lecture will be delivered in the school *auditorium*. (86 私醫)

autobiography 〔 ˌɔtəbaɪ'ɑgrəfɪ 〕 n. 自傳

In his *autobiography*, he mentioned how he was influenced by his teacher. (81 逢甲)

autonomy 〔ɔ'tɑnəmɪ〕 *n.* 自治

Many former colonial possessions in Africa
have achieved a state of
autonomy. (81 文化)

auto	+	nomy
self	+	rule

award 〔ə'wɔrd〕 *n.* 獎

It is not winning the *awards* but the sense
of accomplishment that he enjoys. (88，86 台大)

awareness 〔ə'wɛrnɪs〕 *n.* 意識

Since the incident, people's *awareness* of
environmental protection has been aroused.
(85 交大)

B b

bandage 〔'bændɪdʒ〕 *n.* 繃帶

You'd better put a *bandage*
on that cut finger. (83 淡江)

band	+	age
bind	+	*n.*

bandit 〔'bændɪt 〕 *n.* 強盜

They were attacked by a pack of *bandits* in the desert. (81 淡江)

battle 〔'bætḷ 〕 *n.* 戰鬥

Major Peterson is a veteran who has fought several *battles* in his life. (84 成大)

bilingual 〔 baɪ'lɪŋgwəl 〕 *n.* 能說雙語的人

John can speak two languages; he is a *bilingual*. (84 淡江)

bi + lingual
two + language

blossom 〔'blɑsəm 〕 *n.* 花

The falling *blossoms* floated gently through the air like snowflakes. (86 中原)

bodyguard 〔'bɑdɪˌgɑrd 〕 *n.* 保鑣

The governor was accompanied by two *bodyguards*. (83 文化)

bottom 〔'bɑtəm 〕 *n.* 底部

In the *bottom* of the well they found a
hidden passageway. (85 交大)

breakthrough 〔'brek,θru 〕 *n.* 突破

Scientists have attributed the recent
breakthrough to pure luck. (81 交大)

brochure 〔 bro'ʃjʊr 〕 *n.* 小冊子

The Wangs went to the travel agency for
some *brochures*. (84 政大)

bruise 〔 bruz 〕 *n.* 瘀傷

To treat *bruises*, press with a clean, cold cloth
and follow with a gentle massage. (81 淡江)

burglar 〔'bɝglə 〕 *n.* 夜賊

The store on the corner was robbed last
night by a *burglar*. (83 淡江)

C c

candidate 〔'kændə,det〕 *n.* 候選人

All the *candidates* seemed equally qualified.
It will be a tough race. (86 逢甲)

capacity 〔kə'pæsətɪ〕 *n.* 容量

The *capacity* of the elevator is 1000
kilograms, or 15 people. (86 逢甲)

capital 〔'kæpətḷ〕 *n.* 資金

Lacking *capital*, he applied to the bank for
a loan. (86 成大)

capsule 〔'kæpsḷ〕 *n.* 膠囊

I can't swallow the *capsules* without water.
(86 成大)

castle 〔'kæsḷ〕 *n.* 城堡

Part of the *castle* was destroyed in the war
and later it was reconstructed. (85 台大)

·Check List·

( ) 1. approval   A. thief

( ) 2. aptitude   B. talent ; ability

( ) 3. aroma   C. tablet ; pill

( ) 4. award   D. consciousness

( ) 5. awareness   E. robber

( ) 6. bandage   F. nominee

( ) 7. bandit   G. chateau

( ) 8. battle   H. combat ; fight

( ) 9. brochure   I. booklet

( )10. burglar   J. consent

( )11. candidate   K. dressing

( )12. capacity   L. prize ; medal

( )13. capital   M. volume ; size

( )14. capsule   N. fragrance

( )15. castle   O. funds ; money

Vocabulary Ratings

5–7 *Good*   8–11 *Very Good*   12–15 *Excellent*

Synonyms

1. approval
   = consent
   = agreement

2. aptitude
   = talent
   = gift

3. aroma
   = fragrance
   = odor

4. award
   = prize
   = medal

5. awareness
   = consciousness

6. bandage
   = dressing

7. bandit
   = robber

8. battle
   = combat

9. brochure
   = booklet

10. burglar
    = thief

11. candidate
    = nominee

12. capacity
    = volume

13. capital
    = funds

14. capsule
    = tablet
    = pill

15. castle
    = chateau

catastrophe〔kəˈtæstrəfɪ〕 *n.* 大災難

The nuclear accident at Chernobyl caused an ecological *catastrophe*.

（84淡江）

cata	+ strophe
down	+ *turning*

category 〔ˈkætəˌgɔrɪ〕 *n.* 種類

Dieticians divide food into several *categories*. （89輔大，88政大，87台大，85淡江）

caution 〔ˈkɔʃən〕 *n.* 謹慎

The student answered the question his teacher asked with *caution*. （85中興，82文化）

celebrity 〔səˈlɛbrətɪ〕 *n.* 名人

A stream of *celebrities* could be seen arriving at the award ceremony. （86逢甲）

challenge 〔ˈtʃælɪndʒ〕 *n.* 挑戰

Joining in the race is one of the biggest *challenges* he has ever faced. （86中興）

champion 〔'tʃæmpɪən 〕 *n.* 冠軍

The U.S. team remained the *champion* of
the tournament for three years. (83 文化)

character 〔'kærɪktə 〕 *n.* 品格

He really has a lovely *character*; it's a
shame he's leaving. (86 逢甲)

characteristic 〔,kærɪktə'rɪstɪk 〕 *n.* 特色

One *characteristic* of this computer that I
appreciate very much is its speed.

(88 銘傳，86 中原)

charity 〔'tʃærətɪ 〕 *n.* 慈善

Charity is an important virtue to cultivate.

(86、85 台大，85 交大)

chauffeur 〔'ʃofə，ʃo'fɝ 〕 *n.* 司機

After the party, he asked his *chauffeur* to
drive him home. (86 台大)

chore〔tʃɔr〕 *n.* 雜事

George and Mary shared the household
chores between them. (86 清大)

colleague〔'kɑlig〕 *n.* 同事

Professor Lee is a *colleague* of Professor
Pan. (85 銘傳)

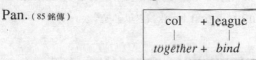

col	+ league
together + *bind*

coma〔'komə〕 *n.* 昏迷

Medical authorities disagree on how to treat
patients who are permanently in a *coma*.
(85 銘傳)

combination〔ˌkɑmbə'neʃən〕 *n.* 結合

The *combination* of alcohol and sleeping
pills was responsible for his death. (86 逢甲)

com	+ bin(e)	+ ation
together +	*two* +	*n.*

comedy 〔'kɑmədɪ 〕 *n.* 喜劇

The actor likes working in *comedy* because he loves to make people laugh. (88 淡江)

comment 〔'kɑmɛnt 〕 *n.* 評論

The critic was asked to make a *comment* on his latest book. (85 中興，82 台大)

commercial 〔 kə'mɝʃəl 〕 *n.* 廣告

After watching the *commercial*, she bought that product because it offered a free gift.

(85 文化，83 東吳)

commission 〔 kə'mɪʃən 〕 *n.* 佣金

The real estate agents' *commission* is 15% of the selling price. (86 逢甲)

committee 〔 kə'mɪtɪ 〕 *n.* 委員會

The planning *committee* is made up of 15 members. (86 逢甲)

compassion 〔 kəm'pæʃən 〕 *n.* 同情

Let's learn to have *compassion* for those who fail. (83 交大，82 文化)

com	+	pass	+	ion
|		|		|
together	+	*feelings*	+	*n.*

competition 〔 ,kampə'tɪʃən 〕 *n.* 比賽

Their son is aggressive. He likes to join in different kinds of *competitions*.

(86 中興，85 東吳)

compliment 〔 'kampləmənt 〕 *n.* 稱讚

He receives many *compliments* on his service and performance. (86 逢甲、私醫，82 成大，80 中興)

comprehension 〔͵kɑmprɪ'hɛnʃən 〕

n. 了解

The questions are designed to test the reading *comprehension* of the students. (89輔大，80中興)

com	+ prehens	+ ion
all	+ *seize*	+ *n.*

concentration 〔͵kɑnsṇ'treʃən 〕 *n.* 專心

The task requires your full *concentration*.

(86逢甲)

concession 〔 kən'sɛʃən 〕 *n.* 讓步

After the boss made some *concessions*, the workers agreed to return to the job. (86成大)

con	+ cess	+ ion
together	+ *go*	+ *n.*

Check List

( )	1. catastrophe	A. blend
( )	2. category	B. sort ; kind
( )	3. caution	C. board
( )	4. character	D. attention
( )	5. characteristic	E. disaster
( )	6. colleague	F. praise
( )	7. combination	G. coworker
( )	8. comment	H. remark
( )	9. compassion	I. carefulness
( )	10. competition	J. sympathy
( )	11. compliment	K. feature
( )	12. comprehension	L. understanding
( )	13. concentration	M. giving way
( )	14. concession	N. contest
( )	15. committee	O. personality

Vocabulary Ratings

5–7 *Good*   8–11 *Very Good*   12–15 *Excellent*

·Synonyms·

1. concentration
   = attention

2. category
   = sort
   = type

3. caution
   = carefulness

4. character
   = personality

5. characteristic
   = feature
   = trait

6. comprehension
   = understanding

7. combination
   = blend
   = mixture

8. comment
   = remark

9. committee
   = board

10. compassion
    = sympathy

11. competition
    = contest

12. compliment
    = praise

13. colleague
    = coworker

14. catastrophe
    = disaster

15. concession
    = giving way
    = yielding

condition〔kən'dɪʃən〕*n.* 情況

The *conditions* in that country have improved a lot in the last ten years.（86 逢甲，85 中興）

conference〔'kɑnfərəns〕*n.* 會議

There is a national *conference* on cancer in New York.（86 中原，84 私醫）

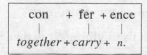

```
con   + fer + ence          con    + flict
 |        |     |             |         |
together +carry+ n.        together + strike
```

conflict〔'kɑnflɪkt〕*n.* 衝突

The *conflict* between them lasted for weeks until he apologized.（86 中興）

congestion〔kən'dʒɛstʃən〕*n.* 阻塞

An inexperienced driver may cause traffic *congestion*.（83 交大，81 東吳）

connection 〔kə'nɛkʃən〕 *n.* 關聯

Scientists have confirmed the *connection* between smoking and cancer. (87 中央，86 中興)

conscience 〔'kanʃəns〕 *n.* 良心

I want to run away, but my *conscience* bothers me. (80 淡江)

consequence 〔'kansə,kwɛns〕 *n.* 結果

If the past has taught us anything, it is that every action has a *consequence*. (84 淡江)

con	+ sequ	+ ence
together	+ *follow*	+ *n.*

conservation 〔,kansə'veʃən〕 *n.* 保育

Animal lovers are making every effort for the *conservation* of endangered species.

(86 逢甲)

con	+ serv	+ ation
all	+ *keep*	+ *n.*

consideration 〔 kən,sɪdə'reʃən 〕 *n.* 考慮

We will take your proposal into *consideration* when we have a discussion. (86 中興)

construction 〔 kən'strʌkʃən 〕 *n.* 建築

The new railroad is still under *construction*. It will be completed next year. (89 成大，86 逢甲)

```
con + struct + ion
 |      |      |
all + build +  n.
```

contentment 〔 kən'tɛntmənt 〕 *n.* 滿足

Happiness lies in *contentment*. (85 東吳)

continent 〔'kɑntənənt 〕 *n.* 大陸

North and South America were referred to as the New *Continents*. (83 淡江)

contribution 〔͵kɑntrə'bjuʃən 〕 n. 貢獻

I make a *contribution* to the charity organization regularly. (85 交大、中興)

```
con  +    tribut    + ion
 |         |          |
all  + bestow (贈與) +  n.
```

conviction 〔 kən'vɪkʃən 〕 n. 信念

He has so much *conviction* in his beliefs that nothing can stop him. (87 中原，86 逢甲)

cooperation 〔 ko͵ɑpə'reʃən 〕 n. 合作

The success of the project was due to everyone's *cooperation*. (88 政大)

core 〔 kor 〕 n. 核心

The pear was rotten to the *core*. (85 交大)

costume 〔'kɑstjum 〕 n. 服裝

All the party goers were asked to dress in 18th century *costume*. (88 中原，86 清大)

counsel 〔'kɑʊnsḷ 〕 n. 諮詢

The suspect declined to accept the legal *counsel*. (83 文化)

coupon 〔'kupɑn 〕 n. 折價卷

This *coupon* is good for a 30 percent discount on your next purchase. (85 中興)

crack 〔 kræk 〕 n. 裂縫

I noticed a *crack* in the cup; you had better throw it away. (86 中原)

criminal 〔'krɪmənḷ 〕 n. 罪犯

The police suspect that the *criminal* might still be at large. (84 交大)

crisis (ˈkraɪsɪs) *n.* 危機

We might have passed the *crisis* safely if we had acted sooner. (86 中興)

curiosity (ˌkjʊrɪˈɑsətɪ) *n.* 好奇心

Do you know that *curiosity* killed the cat? Don't ask too many questions. (85 私醫)

currency (ˈkɝənsɪ) *n.* 貨幣

Devaluation is an official decrease in the par value of a nation's *currency*. (81 中興)

D d

decoration (ˌdɛkəˈreʃən) *n.* 裝飾

The *decorations* Mrs. Daniels put up in the room looked very beautiful. (86 逢甲)

dedication (ˌdɛdəˈkeʃən) *n.* 奉獻

We thank Ms. Kyle for her *dedication* to our institute. (80 淡江)

Check List

( ) 1. condition   A. devotion

( ) 2. conference   B. reflection

( ) 3. conflict   C. outcome

( ) 4. congestion   D. clash

( ) 5. connection   E. outfit

( ) 6. consequence   F. satisfaction

( ) 7. consideration   G. adornment

( ) 8. contentment   H. faith ; belief

( ) 9. conviction   I. association

( ) 10. costume   J. offender

( ) 11. counsel   K. blocking

( ) 12. crack   L. session

( ) 13. criminal   M. advice

( ) 14. decoration   N. state

( ) 15. dedication   O. fracture

Vocabulary Ratings

5–7 *Good*   8–11 *Very Good*   12–15 *Excellent*

·Synonyms·

1. condition
   = state

2. conference
   = session
   = meeting

3. conflict
   = clash

4. congestion
   = blocking

5. connection
   = association
   = link

6. consequence
   = outcome
   = result

7. conviction
   = faith
   = belief

8. consideration
   = reflection

9. contentment
   = satisfaction

10. costume
    = outfit

11. counsel
    = advice
    = suggestion

12. crack
    = fracture

13. criminal
    = offender

14. decoration
    = adornment

15. dedication
    = devotion

defect〔dɪˈfɛkt , ˈdifɛkt〕*n.* 缺點

In his mind, his girlfriend is like a goddess.
He can't find any *defect* in her.

（86、85 銘傳，82 交大）

deficiency〔dɪˈfɪʃənsɪ〕*n.* 不足

A *deficiency* in zinc can cause birth defects
in rodents.（86 銘傳）

de	+ fic	+ ency
down	+ do	+ *n.*

delight〔dɪˈlaɪt〕*n.* 高興

To his parents' *delight*, he was admitted to
National Taiwan University.（88 中央，85 文化）

depreciation〔dɪˌpriʃɪˈeʃən〕*n.* 貶值

The *depreciation* of the currency means
that it is worth less now.（88 中央）

de	+ preci	+ at(e)	+ ion
down	+ price	+ *v.*	+ *n.*

depression 〔 dɪ'prɛʃən 〕 *n.* 憂鬱

After the failure, he was in a state of deep *depression*. (85 私醫)

descendant 〔 dɪ'sɛndənt 〕 *n.* 子孫

His *descendants* settled in the countryside around the city. (83 文化)

```
de  + scend + ant
 |      |      |
down + climb + 人
```

description 〔 dɪ'skrɪpʃən 〕 *n.* 敘述

Many critics praised the detailed and vivid *descriptions* in the novel. (84 東吳)

destination 〔 ˌdɛstə'neʃən 〕 *n.* 目的地

They wanted to drive to Chicago, but because of the storm, they didn't reach their *destination*. (86 逢甲, 81 文化)

determination ﹝ dɪ͵tɝmə'neʃən ﹞ *n.* 決心

It takes courage and *determination* to
succeed in this profession. (86私醫)

device ﹝ dɪ'vaɪs ﹞ *n.* 裝置

You have to read the directions before
operating the complicated *device*. (82輔大)

diabetes ﹝͵daɪə'bitɪs ﹞ *n.* 糖尿病

My grandmother was found to have
diabetes. (88、87中央)

dialect ﹝'daɪəlɛkt ﹞ *n.* 方言

Taiwanese is a major *dialect* spoken in
Taiwan. (83淡江)

disciple ﹝ dɪ'saɪpḷ ﹞ *n.* 弟子

Bruce Lee was the world's most famous
disciple of the martial arts. (85銘傳，81政大)

discount 〔'dɪskaʊnt 〕 *n.* 折扣

We offer a 10% *discount* if you pay in cash.

（86文化）

display 〔 dɪ'sple 〕 *n.* 展示

Ice Age fossils from the Alps are now on *display* in the Natural Science Museum.

（86中正、銘傳，85交大）

disposition 〔ˌdɪspə'zɪʃən 〕 *n.* 性情

Miss Knight was an elegant lady with a gentle *disposition*. （80中興）

distress 〔 dɪ'strɛs 〕 *n.* 痛苦

The *distress* of losing her cat was too much for her to bear. （85銘傳）

diversity 〔 dəˈvɝsətɪ 〕 *n.* 多樣

The *diversity* of colleges in this country indicates that many levels of ability are being considered. (86 交大，85 中興，84 台北大)

```
di   + vers + ity
|       |      |
apart + turn + n.
```

dogma 〔ˈdɔgmə 〕 *n.* 教條

He simply repeats church *dogma* like a parrot with no opinions of his own. (86 中興)

donation 〔 doˈneʃən 〕 *n.* 捐贈

At the end of the service, they passed around a plate for *donations*.
(85 交大)

```
don + ation
|      |
give +  n.
```

donor 〔ˈdonɚ 〕 *n.* 捐贈者

The organs came from an unidentified *donor*. (86 私醫)

drain 〔 dren 〕 *n.* 水管

I must call the plumber because the *drain*
of my sink has become stopped up. (82 靜宜)

duration 〔 djʊˈreʃən 〕 *n.* 期間

The *duration* of a memory varies from
person to person. (90 輔大)

dur + ation
| |
last + *n.*

E e

edge 〔 εdʒ 〕 *n.* 邊緣

The cup fell off the *edge* of the table. (86 台大)

effect 〔 ɪˈfεkt 〕 *n.* 影響

TV commercials have a great *effect* on us
when we decide to buy something. (86 交大)

·Check List·

( ) 1. defect   A. account

( ) 2. deficiency   B. shortage

( ) 3. depreciation   C. doctrine

( ) 4. depression   D. deduction

( ) 5. descendant   E. contribution

( ) 6. description   F. shortcoming

( ) 7. discount   G. verge

( ) 8. display   H. exhibition

( ) 9. disposition   I. anguish

( ) 10. distress   J. offspring

( ) 11. diversity   K. variety

( ) 12. dogma   L. devaluation

( ) 13. donation   M. influence

( ) 14. edge   N. temperament

( ) 15. effect   O. dejection

Vocabulary Ratings

5–7 *Good*   8–11 *Very Good*   12–15 *Excellent*

·Synonyms·

1. defect
   = shortcoming
   = weakness

2. deficiency
   = shortage

3. depreciation
   = devaluation

4. depression
   = dejection

5. descendant
   = offspring

6. description
   = account

7. discount
   = deduction

8. display
   = exhibition

9. disposition
   = temperament
   = personality

10. distress
    = anguish
    = agony

11. diversity
    = variety

12. dogma
    = doctrine
    = creed

13. donation
    = contribution

14. edge
    = verge

15. effect
    = influence
    = impact

efficiency 〔 ə'fɪʃənsɪ 〕 *n.* 效率

They purchased some new machines, hoping
to raise the *efficiency* of production.

（88 政大，85 淡江）

ef	+ fic	+ ency
out	+ *do*	+ *n.*

emphasis 〔'ɛmfəsɪs 〕 *n.* 強調

His parents put much *emphasis* on music
education and sent him to music class. （84 東吳）

endurance 〔 ɪn'djʊrəns 〕 *n.* 耐力

A long-distance runner must have
endurance. （82 逢甲）

en	+ dur	+ ance
in	+ *last*	+ *n.*

enthusiasm 〔 ɪn'θjuzɪˌæzəm 〕 *n.* 熱誠

George spoke about the new project with
enthusiasm. （83 輔大）

entry 〔'ɛntrɪ〕 *n.* 進入

The university plans to raise *entry* standards.

（83文化）

epidemic 〔,ɛpə'dɛmɪk〕 *n.* 傳染病

The AIDS *epidemic* is a major problem in
Africa and parts of Asia. （86中興，81淡江）

epi	+	dem	+	ic
among	+	people	+	*n.*

erosion 〔ɪ'roʒən〕 *n.* 侵蝕

Caves are often formed by selective *erosion*
of cliffs by the sea. （85私醫）

errand 〔'ɛrənd〕 *n.* 差事

John likes to help his mother. He often runs
errands for her. （87東吳）

eruption 〔 ɪ'rʌpʃən 〕 *n.* 爆發

The volcanic *eruption* in the area forced
local people to evacuate. (88中央)

e	+	rupt	+	ion
		|		|
out	+	*break*	+	*n.*

estate 〔 ə'stet 〕 *n.* 地產

Mr. Chen's real *estate* downtown is worth
3.6 million dollars. (86逢甲)

esteem 〔 ə'stim 〕 *n.* 尊敬

He lowered himself in our *esteem* by his
foolish behavior. (82淡江)

euthanasia 〔 ˌjuθə'neʒə 〕 *n.* 安樂死

Euthanasia is a very controversial issue in
many societies.

(83淡江)

eu	+	thanas	+	ia
		|		|
well	+	*die*	+	*n.*

evaluation 〔 ɪˌvæljʊˈeʃən 〕 *n.* 評估

The committee hasn't finished its *evaluation* of the workers' demands. (86 逢甲)

evidence 〔ˈɛvədəns 〕 *n.* 證據

Astronomers have found the first *evidence* that gravity waves exist.

（88 政大，86 清大、逢甲，85 中興，82 輔大）

```
e   + vid + ence
|      |      |
out + see  +  n.
```

exaggeration 〔 ɪgˌzædʒəˈreʃən 〕 *n.* 誇張

In literature, verbal *exaggeration* sometimes can achieve comic and often satiric effects.

（84 私醫）

execution 〔 ˌɛksɪˈkjuʃən 〕 *n.* 執行

Public administration consists of the *execution* of public policy by public authorities. (86 中興)

exhibition 〔͵ɛksə'bɪʃən 〕 *n.* 展覽會

There will an *exhibition* of her works at the museum next month. (85 交大)

expense 〔 ɪk'spɛns 〕 *n.* 費用

The *expense* of rebuilding the business drained all his remaining capital. (86 政大)

extension 〔 ɪk'stɛnʃən 〕 *n.* 延伸

The politician did everything for the *extension* of his influence. (85 文化、私醫)

ex	+	tens	+ ion
out	+	*stretch*	+ *n.*

extinction 〔 ɪk'stɪŋkʃən 〕 *n.* 絕種

Some scientists attributed the *extinction* of dinosaurs to meteors. (85 文化)

F f

facility 〔 fə'sɪlətɪ 〕 *n.* 設施

At most schools, *facilities* for learning and
recreation are available to students.

（86銘傳，81逢甲）

```
fac + il(e) + ity
 |      |      |
 do  + adj. +  n.
```

fantasy 〔'fæntəsɪ 〕 *n.* 幻想

I would love to travel to the moon, but I
know that is just a *fantasy*. （86中興）

fatigue 〔 fə'tig 〕 *n.* 疲倦

He felt asleep soon owing to *fatigue*.

（86政大，85銘傳，83中興）

fee 〔 fi 〕 *n.* 費用

You must pay a yearly *fee* in order to remain
a member of the club. （86台大）

•Check List•

( ) 1. emphasis   A. assessment

( ) 2. endurance   B. fancy

( ) 3. enthusiasm   C. exhausion

( ) 4. erosion   D. proof

( ) 5. eruption   E. stress

( ) 6. esteem   F. mercy killing

( ) 7. euthanasia   G. durability

( ) 8. evaluation   H. overstatement

( ) 9. evidence   I. regard

( ) 10. exaggeration   J. eagerness

( ) 11. execution   K. performance

( ) 12. extinction   L. payment

( ) 13. fantasy   M. outburst

( ) 14. fatigue   N. extermination

( ) 15. fee   O. wearing away

Vocabulary Ratings

5–7 *Good*   8–11 *Very Good*   12–15 *Excellent*

·Synonyms·

1. emphasis
   = stress

2. endurance
   = durability

3. enthusiasm
   = eagerness
   = zest

4. erosion
   = wearing away

5. exaggeration
   = overstatement

6. euthanasia
   = mercy killing

7. evidence
   = proof

8. evaluation
   = assessment

9. eruption
   = outburst

10. esteem
    = regard
    = reverence

11. execution
    = performance

12. extinction
    = extermination

13. fantasy
    = fancy
    = imagination

14. fatigue
    = exhausion
    = weariness

15. fee
    = payment
    = charge

fiction〔'fɪkʃən〕 *n.* 小說

As a proverb goes, "Truth is sometimes stranger than *fiction*." (87 逢甲，81 台大)

fidelity〔fə'dɛlətɪ〕 *n.* 忠實

Henry's *fidelity* is beyond question; he always fulfills his obligations.

（86 政大）

```
fidel + ity
  |      |
trust + n.
```

flattery〔'flætərɪ〕 *n.* 諂媚

His praise of my artwork was just *flattery*; I know he didn't really like it. (86 私醫)

flaw〔flɔ〕 *n.* 裂縫

Small *flaws* in an object show that it is man-made. (84 台北大)

function〔'fʌŋkʃən〕 *n.* 功能

The *function* of an alarm clock is to wake people up at a certain time. (88 銘傳)

G g

glimpse 〔 glɪmps 〕 *n.* 一瞥

While traveling, we caught *glimpses* of
some desert animals. (87 輔大)

gossip 〔'gɑsəp 〕 *n.* 閒聊

Although the *gossip* about her is not true,
everyone believes the story. (85 銘傳)

gratitude 〔'grætə,tjud 〕 *n.* 感激

I sent her flowers and a thank-you note to
show my *gratitude* to her.

(88 政大)

grat	+ itude
please +	*n.*

grief 〔 grif 〕 *n.* 悲傷

Albert was too mature to display his *grief*
in public. (81 清大)

guarantee 〔ˌgærən'ti 〕 *n.* 保證

All of the appliances purchased at our store have a one year *guarantee*. (85 淡江)

gymnasium 〔 dʒɪm'nezɪəm 〕 *n.* 體育館

The volleyball game will be held in the *gymnasium* this afternoon. (86 私醫)

H h

habitat 〔'hæbəˌtæt 〕 *n.* 棲息地

People have destroyed the natural *habitat* of many species. (86 輔大)

hardship 〔'hɑrdʃɪp 〕 *n.* 艱苦

The soldiers bore many *hardships* during the war. (88 輔大)

harvest〔'hɑrvɪst〕 *n.* 收穫

The rice *harvest* is poor this year because of the drought.（86 輔大）

hazard〔'hæzəd〕 *n.* 危險

The brave hero faced all *hazards* without flinching.（89 輔大，87 中原，86 私醫，84 交大、成大）

headline〔'hɛd,laɪn〕 *n.* 標題

The *headline* was so interesting that I decided to read the story right away.

（86 中原）

helmet〔'hɛlmɪt〕 *n.* 頭盔

If you ride a motorcycle without a *helmet*, you will be fined.（85 中興）

heredity 〔 həˈrɛdətɪ 〕 n. 遺傳

His height is due to *heredity*. His father is also very tall. (88 中原)

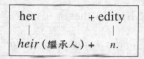

```
her          + edity
 |              |
heir (繼承人) +  n.
```

hint 〔 hɪnt 〕 n. 提示

I'll give you a *hint*, since you don't remember. (86 輔大)

hostility 〔 hɑsˈtɪlətɪ 〕 n. 敵意

There is a great deal of *hostility* between the two boys and they often fight. (81 交大)

hurricane 〔 ˈhɝɪ͵ken 〕 n. 颶風

Every year *hurricanes* damage thousands of dollars worth of property. (85 銘傳)

hypothesis 〔 haɪ'pɑθəsɪs 〕 *n.* 假說

We can test our *hypothesis* by performing an experiment in the lab. (86 成大)

```
hypo  +  thes  +   (s)is
  |        |         |
under  +  put  + condition
```

I i

identity 〔 aɪ'dɛntətɪ 〕 *n.* 身分

The student card sometimes can be used to prove your *identity*. (86 中興、文化)

image 〔'ɪmɪdʒ 〕 *n.* 影像

A dream usually consists of visual *images* that tell a story. (85 輔大)

impact 〔'ɪmpækt 〕 *n.* 影響

The new law will have a great *impact* on the government policy makers. (86 清大)

•Check List•

(   ) 1. fidelity   A. loyalty

(   ) 2. glimpse   B. warranty

(   ) 3. gossip   C. typhoon

(   ) 4. gratitude   D. effect

(   ) 5. grief   E. difficulty

(   ) 6. guarantee   F. glance

(   ) 7. hardship   G. assumption

(   ) 8. harvest   H. crop

(   ) 9. hazard   I. enmity

(   ) 10. headline   J. sorrow

(   ) 11. hint   K. chat

(   ) 12. hostility   L. danger

(   ) 13. hurricane   M. appreciation

(   ) 14. hypothesis   N. clue

(   ) 15. impact   O. title

Vocabulary Ratings

5–7 *Good*   8–11 *Very Good*   12–15 *Excellent*

Synonyms

1. fidelity
   = loyalty
   = faithfulness

2. glimpse
   = glance

3. gossip
   = chat
   = small talk

4. gratitude
   = appreciation
   = thankfulness

5. grief
   = sorrow

6. guarantee
   = warranty
   = assurance

7. hardship
   = difficulty

8. harvest
   = crop

9. hazard
   = danger

10. headline
    = title

11. hint
    = clue

12. hostility
    = enmity

13. hurricane
    = typhoon
    = cyclone

14. hypothesis
    = assumption

15. impact
    = effect

imperfection 〔͵ɪmpɚˈfɛkʃən 〕 *n.* 不完美

The manager does not tolerate *imperfections* in himself or in others. (85 銘傳，82 交大)

im +	per	+ fect + ion
not +	*thoroughly* +	*do* + *n.*

incentive 〔 ɪnˈsɛntɪv 〕 *n.* 動機

Students who dislike school must be given an *incentive* to learn. (84 台北大)

inclination 〔͵ɪnkləˈneʃən 〕 *n.* 傾向

In ancient China, a woman was not free to follow her own *inclination*, even in the matter of marriage. (88 台大，85 淡江，80 逢甲)

in +	clin(e)	+ ation
toward +	*lean* (靠) +	*n.*

index 〔'ɪndɛks 〕 *n.* 索引

When looking for a word in the book, you can look it up in the *index* first. (81 中興)

infection 〔ɪn'fɛkʃən 〕 *n.* 感染

The doctor said I had a mild *infection* and gave me some pills to take.

(89 輔大，87 逢甲，85 銘傳)

inhabitant 〔ɪn'hæbətənt 〕 *n.* 居民

Years ago the *inhabitants* of the town fought for the right to collect their own taxes.

(82 政大)

innovation 〔͵ɪnə'veʃən 〕 *n.* 創新

The automobile was an *innovation* that changed the way people lived. (85 逢甲)

```
in  + nov  + ation
 |      |       |
in  + new  +   n.
```

insecticide 〔 ɪn'sɛktə,saɪd 〕 n. 殺蟲劑

DDT is generally considered an effective *insecticide*. (82 文化)

insect + icide
昆蟲 + *kill*

insight 〔'ɪn,saɪt 〕 n. 洞察力

Charlie is a man of *insight*, observant of every detail around him. (87 文化)

insomnia 〔 ɪn'sɑmnɪə 〕 n. 失眠

When a man suffers from severe *insomnia*, he is likely to be listless. (88、87 中央、86 清大、82 中興)

in + somn + ia
not + *sleep* + *n.*

installment 〔 ɪn'stɔlmənt 〕 n. 分期付款

I could not afford to pay for the car all at once, so I pay an *installment* every month. (85 銘傳)

intelligence 〔 ɪn'tɛlədʒəns 〕 n. 智力

It was not *intelligence* but diligence that led
to his success.

（88、87 政大）

intel	+	lig	+ ence
between	+	choose	+ *n.*

intention 〔 ɪn'tɛnʃən 〕 n. 意圖

He went to Paris with the *intention* of
learning French well. （85 逢甲）

interpretation 〔 ɪn,tɜprɪ'teʃən 〕 n. 詮釋

Every contestant will play the same piece
of music, and they will be judged on their
interpretation of it. （90 輔大，86 成大）

intuition 〔 ,ɪntu'ɪʃən 〕 n. 直覺

Don't ask why I felt that way. It was my
intuition. （80 淡江）

in	+	tui	+ tion
in	+	watch	+ *n.*

J j

jackpot 〔'dʒæk͵pɑt 〕 *n.* 累積獎金

The old lady bought a lottery ticket and hit the *jackpot*. (85 清大)

journalist 〔'dʒɝnḷɪst 〕 *n.* 記者

Peter is a *journalist* with the magazine "Around the World." (88 銘傳)

L l

legend 〔'lɛdʒənd 〕 *n.* 傳說

According to the local *legend*, the hero defeated the monster and saved all the villagers. (88 中正)

leisure 〔'liʒɚ 〕 *n.* 閒暇

This relaxing trip is good for the man who loves *leisure*. (85 清大)

M m

magnitude 〔'mægnə,tjud 〕 *n.* 強度

The earthquake of great *magnitude*
destroyed several buildings.

（86 清大）

magn + itude
| |
great + *n.*

margin 〔'mɑrdʒɪn 〕 *n.* 頁邊空白

My teacher wrote a comment in the *margin*
of my paper. （86 台大）

mass 〔 mæs 〕 *n.* 大眾

The *mass* rapid transit system in Taipei is
very convenient. （85 交大）

maxim 〔'mæksɪm 〕 *n.* 格言

My *maxim* is "no pains, no gains." （82 文化）

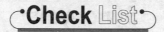

Check List

( ) 1. imperfection   A. faultiness

( ) 2. incentive   B. origination

( ) 3. inclination   C. intellect

( ) 4. infection   D. reporter

( ) 5. inhabitant   E. vision

( ) 6. innovation   F. motivation

( ) 7. insight   G. spare time

( ) 8. insomnia   H. sleeplessness

( ) 9. intelligence   I. instinct

( )10. interpretation   J. tendency

( )11. intuition   K. resident

( )12. journalist   L. scale

( )13. leisure   M. explanation

( )14. magnitude   N. contagion

( )15. maxim   O. motto

Vocabulary Ratings

5–7 *Good*   8–11 *Very Good*   12–15 *Excellent*

·Synonyms·

1. imperfection
   = faultiness
   = defectiveness

2. incentive
   = motivation

3. inclination
   = tendency

4. infection
   = contagion

5. innovation
   = origination

6. maxim
   = motto

7. insomnia
   = sleeplessness

8. intelligence
   = intellect

9. interpretation
   = explanation

10. intuition
    = instinct
    = hunch

11. journalist
    = reporter

12. leisure
    = spare time

13. magnitude
    = scale
    = degree

14. inhabitant
    = resident
    = dweller

15. insight
    = vision
    = perception

medication [ˌmɛdɪˈkeʃən] *n.* 藥物治療

With good *medication*, she is recovering little by little. (87東吳)

mercy [ˈmɝsɪ] *n.* 慈悲

The convicted robber begged the judge for *mercy* because he did not want to go to jail.

(87中央，86政大)

mine [maɪn] *n.* 寶庫

That set of reference books is a rich *mine* of information. (86私醫)

mineral [ˈmɪnərəl] *n.* 礦物

Gold is a very valuable *mineral*. (80淡江)

missionary [ˈmɪʃənˌɛrɪ] *n.* 傳教士

Many *missionaries* are highly respected for their kindness.

(86銘傳)

mis	+ sion	+ ary
|	|	|
send	+ *n.*	+ 人

monopoly 〔 məˈnɑplɪ 〕 *n.* 獨占

The phone company lost its *monopoly* when the market was opened to other competitors.

（88 銘傳）

mono	+ poly
sole（單獨的）	+ *sell*

motivation 〔,motəˈveʃən 〕 *n.* 動機

Motivation is a primary factor in learning.

（83 輔大，80 中興）

mystery 〔ˈmɪstrɪ 〕 *n.* 神秘

What exists outside of our galaxy is still a *mystery*. （81 台大）

N n

necessity 〔 nəˈsɛsətɪ 〕 *n.* 必需品

Food, drink, clothing and a roof over one's head — these are the daily *necessities* that no one can do without. （84 政大）

nomination (ˌnɑməˈneʃən) *n.* 提名

The politician happily accepted the
nomination for president and promised
to do his best to win the election. (87 交大)

```
nomin + at(e) + ion
  |       |       |
name  +   v.  +   n.
```

nostalgia (nɑˈstældʒɪə) *n.* 懷舊

During the class reunion, we were filled
with *nostalgia* for our school days. (85 中興)

novelty (ˈnɑvḷtɪ) *n.* 新奇

The children will play with a new toy until
the *novelty* wears off, and then they will
ignore it. (88 政大，85 中興)

nutrient (ˈnjutrɪənt) *n.* 養分

It is important to get the right *nutrients* in
our diet if we want to stay well. (83 交大)

O o

obedience 〔 ə'bidɪəns 〕 n. 服從

Our parents expect *obedience* when they ask us to do something. (86 中興)

obesity 〔 o'bisətɪ 〕 n. 肥胖

Obesity may be the most serious health problem facing Americans today.

(88 中央、輔大，87 中央)

obligation 〔 ,ablə'geʃən 〕 n. 義務

Anyone who causes damage is under *obligation* to pay for it. (86 銘傳)

ob + lig + ation
| | |
to + bind + n.

ob + sta + cle
| | |
against + stand + 物

obstacle 〔 'abstəkḷ 〕 n. 障礙

Impatience is probably his *obstacle* to winning the game. (86 銘傳)

odor 〔'odɚ〕 *n.* 味道

The garbage gives off an unpleasant *odor*.

(85 清大)

offspring 〔'ɔf,sprɪŋ〕 *n.* 子孫

A mother bear will do anything to protect
her *offspring*. (85 政大、交大)

opponent 〔ə'ponənt〕 *n.* 對手

The candidate will not be able to defeat his
opponent in the local election. (88 中正，87 淡江)

op	+ pon + ent
against	+ put + 人

opt	+ ion
wish	+ n.

option 〔'ɑpʃən〕 *n.* 選擇

After graduating from high school, every
student has the *option* of beginning a career
or attending college. (81 政大)

ordeal 〔 ɔr'dil 〕 *n.* 嚴酷的考驗

We felt sorry for the victim's family because
they had to go through such an *ordeal*.

（86 銘傳）

origin 〔'ɔrədʒɪn 〕 *n.* 起源

No one knows the exact *origin* of the tribe,
but most people think they came from the
northern plains. （86 中興、逢甲）

originator 〔 ə'rɪdʒəˌnetɚ 〕 *n.* 創始者

Steven is the *originator* of the plan, so you
should speak to him if you have any
questions. （81 中興）

ornament 〔'ɔrnəmənt 〕 *n.* 裝飾品

Many people like to decorate trees with
ornaments for Christmas.

（85 政大、中興，82 文化）

orn	+ ament
decorate +	*n.*

Check List

(   ) 1. missionary   A. smell ; scent

(   ) 2. mystery   B. secrecy

(   ) 3. necessity   C. source

(   ) 4. nostalgia   D. decoration

(   ) 5. nutrient   E. creator

(   ) 6. obedience   F. preacher

(   ) 7. obesity   G. reminiscence

(   ) 8. obligation   H. alternative

(   ) 9. obstacle   I. overweightness

(   ) 10. odor   J. requirement

(   ) 11. opponent   K. hindrance

(   ) 12. option   L. nourishment

(   ) 13. origin   M. rival ; foe

(   ) 14. originator   N. responsibility

(   ) 15. ornament   O. submission

Vocabulary Ratings

5–7 *Good*   8–11 *Very Good*   12–15 *Excellent*

·Synonyms·

1. necessity
 = requirement

2. nostalgia
 = reminiscence

3. nutrient
 = nourishment
 = nutrition

4. obesity
 = overweightness

5. obligation
 = responsibility

6. obstacle
 = hindrance
 = obstruction

7. mystery
 = secrecy

8. missionary
 = preacher

9. odor
 = smell
 = scent

10. opponent
 = rival
 = foe

11. option
 = alternative
 = choice

12. origin
 = source

13. originator
 = creator

14. obedience
 = submission
 = conformity

15. ornament
 = decoration

outlet 〔'aʊt͵lɛt 〕 *n.* 出口

The fan pulls the steam in the kitchen
through an *outlet* in the roof. (86 中興)

outline 〔'aʊt͵laɪn 〕 *n.* 大綱

My teacher suggested that I write an *outline*
of my main ideas before I try to write the
research paper. (81 中興)

outrage 〔'aʊt͵redʒ 〕 *n.* 憤怒

His *outrage* was evident from the angry
expression on his face. (85 文化)

overdose 〔'ovɚ͵dos 〕 *n.* 用藥過量

If you take too much of the medicine, you
will suffer from an *overdose*. (86 銘傳)

over + dose
| |
over + 劑量

P p

pardon 〔'pɑrdn̩〕 n. 原諒

He didn't hear the message clearly, so he
said, "I beg your *pardon*?" (87東吳)

participation 〔pəˌtɪsə'peʃən〕 n. 參加

The success of the festival depended on
the *participation* of the whole community.
(89文化)

pastime 〔'pæsˌtaɪm〕 n. 娛樂

Tai chi is one of my grandfather's *pastimes*.
(87輔大)

pedestrian 〔pə'dɛstrɪən〕 n. 行人

This representative is very keen on the
rights of *pedestrians*.
(82政大)

pedestr	+	ian
foot	+	人

penalty 〔'pɛnḷtɪ 〕 *n.* 處罰

The extreme *penalty* of the law used to be punishment by death. (88 淡江)

peril 〔'pɛrəl 〕 *n.* 危險

When a war breaks out, many innocent people are in *peril*. (87 逢甲，85 輔大)

permission 〔 pə'mɪʃən 〕 *n.* 允許

You can't read other people's letters without *permission*. (88 政大)

pesticide 〔'pɛstɪ͵saɪd 〕 *n.* 殺蟲劑

The use of *pesticide* may result in green-house effects.

(84 政大，82 逢甲)

pest	+	icide
害蟲	+	*kill*

petition 〔 pəˈtɪʃən 〕 *n.* 請願書

Some citizens signed a *petition* asking the
city government for a new park in their
neighborhood.

(85 中興)

```
pet  + ition
 |      |
seek +  n.
```

phobia 〔ˈfobɪə 〕 *n.* 恐懼症

His fear of flying was more than mere
nervousness; it was a real *phobia*. (84 台北大)

platform 〔ˈplætˌfɔrm 〕 *n.* 講台

The students stood on a *platform* when they
gave their speeches. (85 中興)

pledge 〔 plɛdʒ 〕 *n.* 誓言

The *pledge* of the Declaration of Independence is the promise of "life, liberty and
the pursuit of happiness." (82 淡江)

poll 〔 pol 〕 *n.* 民意測驗

In a 1983 newspaper *poll*, Ann Landers, an advice columnist, was listed among the 25 most influential women in the U.S.

（86 逢甲，84 私醫）

poster 〔'postɚ 〕 *n.* 海報

We put up a *poster* to advertise the school play. （86 台大）

preference 〔'prɛfrəns 〕 *n.* 偏愛

Her *preference* in reading is novels.

（87 政大，86、85 清大）

pre	+	fer	+ ence
before	+	*carry*	+ *n.*

prejudice 〔'prɛdʒədɪs 〕 *n.* 偏見

A referee must be fair and not have any *prejudice* against one of the teams. （86 中興）

pre	+	jud	+ ice
before	+	*judge*	+ *n.*

prescription 〔 prɪˈskrɪpʃən 〕 *n.* 藥方

He lost the *prescription* for the medicine, so he had to go back to the doctor to get another one. (87 中原、淡江)

prestige 〔 prɛsˈtiʒ 〕 *n.* 聲望

Prestige is one of the factors when one chooses a university. (86 逢甲，84 淡江)

prey 〔 pre 〕 *n.* 獵物

Small animals such as mice are *prey* for many kinds of snakes. (86 交大)

pride 〔 praɪd 〕 *n.* 驕傲

He took *pride* in his daughter's achievement. (87 政大，83 中興)

principle 〔ˈprɪnsəp!〕 *n.* 原則

The *principle* that all men are created equal was stated clearly in the Declaration of Independence. (82 成大)

•Check List•

( ) 1. outlet	A. summary
( ) 2. outline	B. consent
( ) 3. outrage	C. punishment
( ) 4. pardon	D. fear
( ) 5. penalty	E. forgiveness
( ) 6. peril	F. vent ; opening
( ) 7. permission	G. fondness
( ) 8. phobia	H. reputation
( ) 9. platform	I. victim ; game
( )10. pledge	J. podium
( )11. poll	K. vow ; oath
( )12. preference	L. bias
( )13. prejudice	M. survey
( )14. prestige	N. danger
( )15. prey	O. fury ; wrath

Vocabulary Ratings

5–7 *Good*   8–11 *Very Good*   12–15 *Excellent*

·Synonyms·

1. outlet
   = vent

2. outline
   = summary
   = sketch

3. outrage
   = fury
   = wrath

4. pardon
   = forgiveness

5. penalty
   = punishment

6. peril
   = danger
   = hazard

7. pledge
   = vow
   = oath

8. permission
   = consent

9. phobia
   = fear

10. platform
    = podium

11. poll
    = survey

12. preference
    = fondness

13. prejudice
    = bias
    = partiality

14. prestige
    = reputation

15. prey
    = victim
    = game

prison (ˈprɪzn̩) *n.* 監獄

The man was found guilty and sent to *prison* for several years. (85台大)

privilege (ˈprɪvlɪdʒ) *n.* 特權

He entered the exclusive club by means of *privilege*.

(88中正)

privi	+ lege
private	+ *law*

procedure (prəˈsidʒɚ) *n.* 程序

The teacher gave us clear instructions for the difficult *procedure*. (85逢甲)

process (ˈprɑsɛs) *n.* 過程

In the *process* of learning to write, one has to learn to think at the same time.

(86輔大，85逢甲，82東吳)

pro	+ cess
forward	+ *go*

productivity 〔͵prodʌk'tɪvətɪ 〕 *n.* 生產力

Productivity in this factory will definitely increase with the use of these new machines.

（83交大）

promotion 〔 prə'moʃən 〕 *n.* 升職

He has been working hard since he came to this company. I think he deserves a *promotion*. （86逢甲）

property 〔'prɑpətɪ 〕 *n.* 財產

They lost a lot of money and they are considering selling their *property*.

（90輔大，86中興）

prosperity 〔 prɑs'pɛrətɪ 〕 *n.* 興盛

The city has enjoyed *prosperity* for the past few years. （87文化）

pro	+ sper	+ ity
forward	+ *hope*	+ *n.*

protest 〔'protɛst 〕 *n.* 抗議

Tomorrow I will take part in a *protest* demonstration. (87 交大)

pursuit 〔 pɚ'sut 〕 *n.* 追求

The cat ran by in *pursuit* of a mouse.

(87 台北大，86 交大，85 中興)

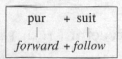

pur	+ suit
forward	+ follow

Q q

quest 〔 kwɛst 〕 *n.* 追求

The *quest* for a humanized society in which people care for real lives rather than machines is intensifying. (86 中興)

R r

rage 〔 redʒ 〕 *n.* 憤怒

My parents flew into a *rage* when they saw my bad grades. (86 私醫)

rebellion 〔 rɪ'bɛljən 〕 *n.* 叛變

A revolt of soldiers or sailors against their superiors is called a *rebellion*. (85 輔大)

re + bell + ion
| | |
again + war + n.

re + reipt
| |
back + take

receipt 〔 rɪ'sit 〕 *n.* 收據

If you want to exchange the item, please return it with its *receipt*. (87 淡江)

recession 〔 rɪ'sɛʃən 〕 *n.* 不景氣

A large number of people are out of work because of the *recession*.

(86 成大)

re + cess + ion
| | |
back + go + n.

recognition 〔 ͵rɛkəg'nɪʃən 〕 *n.* 承認

The scientist received *recognition* for his work at the award ceremony. (85 文化、私醫)

recovery 〔 rɪˈkʌvərɪ 〕 *n.* 恢復

Proper exercise plays a significant role in
the *recovery* of patients with various back
ailments. (84 私醫)

recreation 〔 ͵rɛkrɪˈeʃən 〕 *n.* 娛樂

The *recreation* our whole family take part
in most often is singing karaoke.

(90 輔大，80 淡江)

refugee 〔 ͵rɛfjʊˈdʒi 〕 *n.* 難民

Some *refugees* are forced to abandon their
homeland for political reasons. (80 交大)

```
   re  +  fug        + ee
   |      |            |
  back + flee (逃走) + 人
```

remedy 〔 ˈrɛmədɪ 〕 *n.* 治療方法

Hot tea with honey is a good *remedy* for a
sore throat. (87 淡江)

remorse 〔rɪˈmɔrs〕 n. 後悔

The criminal felt no *remorse* for his crime.

（88 中央，82 清大）

representative 〔ˌrɛprɪˈzɛntətɪv〕 n. 代表

The chairman sent a *representative* to the
meeting because he was unable to attend.

（85 台大）

reputation 〔ˌrɛpjəˈteʃən〕 n. 名聲

He enjoys a high *reputation* as a scholar.

（85 逢甲，80 中興）

reservation 〔ˌrɛzəˈveʃən〕 n. 預訂

Have you made *reservations* for your trip
to Europe yet?（80 淡江）

```
re  + serv + ation
 |      |      |
back + keep +  n.
```

·Check List·

( ) 1. prison   A. possessions

( ) 2. process   B. chase ; quest

( ) 3. promotion   C. acknowledgement

( ) 4. property   D. booking

( ) 5. prosperity   E. jail

( ) 6. protest   F. agent

( ) 7. pursuit   G. treatment

( ) 8. rebellion   H. slump

( ) 9. recession   I. course

( )10. recognition   J. success

( )11. recovery   K. objection

( )12. remedy   L. repentance

( )13. remorse   M. revival

( )14. representative   N. advancement

( )15. reservation   O. revolt

Vocabulary Ratings

5–7 *Good*   8–11 *Very Good*   12–15 *Excellent*

·Synonyms·

1. recognition
   = acknowledgement

2. representative
   = agent

3. promotion
   = advancement

4. property
   = possessions

5. recession
   = slump
   = depression

6. protest
   = objection

7. remorse
   = repentance
   = regret

8. rebellion
   = revolt

9. prosperity
   = success
   = affluence

10. prison
    = jail

11. recovery
    = revival

12. remedy
    = treatment
    = cure

13. pursuit
    = chase
    = quest

14. process
    = course

15. reservation
    = booking

resignation 〔͵rɛzɪg'neʃən〕 *n.* 辭職

The minister's sudden *resignation* surprised us all. (82文化)

re	+ sign + ation
|	| |
again + 簽名 +	*n.*

resource 〔rɪ'sors〕 *n.* 資源

The country is short of natural *resources*.

(88銘傳，87中興，80淡江)

restriction 〔rɪ'strɪkʃən〕 *n.* 限制

Due to the age *restriction*, the child couldn't enter the theater and watch the movie. (80中興)

reward 〔rɪ'wɔrd〕 *n.* 報酬

I gave the boy a *reward* for running an errand for me. (87中原，86台大，85清大)

rival 〔'raɪvḷ〕 *n.* 對手

He shook hands with his *rival* before the match. (88中正，85銘傳，83淡江)

rubbish 〔ˈrʌbɪʃ 〕 *n.* 垃圾

The *rubbish* in your house must be cleared away every day. (84、80中興)

S s

satellite 〔ˈsætḷˌaɪt 〕 *n.* 衛星

Communication *satellites* enable people to watch live broadcasts from anywhere in the world. (86私醫,85淡江)

scene 〔 sin 〕 *n.* 景色

The sun setting over the ocean was a beautiful *scene*. (85文化)

screen 〔 skrin 〕 *n.* 螢幕

We bought a brand-new television set with a 33-inch *screen*. (85文化)

segregation 〔,sɛgrɪ'geʃən 〕 *n.* 種族隔離

Racism of a stronger group against a weaker group often leads to *segregation*. (87 交大,82 政大)

se	+ gregat	+ ion
apart	+ *collect*	+ *n.*

selection 〔 sə'lɛkʃən 〕 *n.* 挑選

In violin making, the *selection* of the wood is crucial.

(86 中原)

se	+ lect	+ ion
apart	+ *choose*	+ *n.*

servant 〔'sɝvənt 〕 *n.* 僕人

Mr. Jenson is very rich and employs five *servants* at his house. (86 台大)

session 〔'sɛʃən 〕 *n.* 開會

You must remain quiet when the court is in *session*. (86 成大)

shelter 〔'ʃɛltɚ〕 *n.* 避難

Many people took *shelter* at the café during the thunderstorm. (81 逢甲)

signal 〔'sɪgnḷ〕 *n.* 信號

He gave me a *signal* to make a right turn here. (86 台大)

signature 〔'sɪgnətʃɚ〕 *n.* 簽名

The manager put his *signature* on the last page of the document. (85 銘傳)

significance 〔sɪg'nɪfəkəns〕 *n.* 重要性

Having the first phase done is of great *significance* to the whole project. (88 中正, 83 淡江)

solitude 〔'sɑləˌtjud〕 *n.* 孤獨

Living alone and never socializing with others, he seems to enjoy *solitude*. (86 逢甲)

sol	+ itude
alone +	*n.*

sorrow ('saro) *n.* 悲傷

To our great *sorrow*, old Mr. Wang passed away last night. (86 輔大)

sort (sort) *n.* 種類

There are two *sorts* of books required for basic bookkeeping. (86 中原)

source (sors) *n.* 來源

The *source* of the Yellow River is located more than two thousand miles from its mouth. (87、86 中興)

spectator ('spɛktetə) *n.* 觀衆

There were many *spectators* at the baseball game. (80 輔大)

spect	+	at(e)	+	or
see	+	*v.*	+	人

status ('stetəs) *n.* 地位

It used to be a *status* symbol to have a
Mercedes Benz.

（86 中興）

```
stat   + us
 |       |
stand  + n.
```

stimulus ('stɪmjələs) *n.* 興奮劑

If you have trouble falling asleep, avoid
too much *stimulus* before you go to bed.

（88 中正，85 清大）

stock (stɑk) *n.* 股票

Mr. El bought some *stocks* in that company
as an investment. （86 台大）

stress (strɛs) *n.* 強調

Traditional parents put much *stress* on the
academic performance of their children.

（86 輔大，85 交大）

Check List

( )	1. resource	A. supply
( )	2. restriction	B. sight ; view
( )	3. reward	C. viewer
( )	4. rubbish	D. importance
( )	5. scene	E. share
( )	6. selection	F. limitation
( )	7. session	G. refuge
( )	8. shelter	H. kind ; type
( )	9. signal	I. choice
( )	10. significance	J. repayment
( )	11. solitude	K. meeting
( )	12. sort	L. garbage ; trash
( )	13. spectator	M. loneliness
( )	14. status	N. sign
( )	15. stock	O. position

Vocabulary Ratings

5–7 *Good*   8–11 *Very Good*   12–15 *Excellent*

·Synonyms·

1. resource
   = supply

2. restriction
   = limitation

3. reward
   = repayment

4. rubbish
   = garbage
   = trash
   = litter

5. scene
   = sight
   = view

6. selection
   = choice

7. shelter
   = refuge
   = haven

8. session
   = meeting

9. signal
   = sign

10. significance
    = importance
    = consequence

11. solitude
    = loneliness

12. sort
    = kind
    = type

13. spectator
    = viewer

14. status
    = position

15. stock
    = share

stroll ﹝ strol ﹞ *n.* 散步

My father is used to taking a *stroll* in the park every day after dinner. (86 清大)

subscription ﹝ səb'skrɪpʃən ﹞ *n.* 訂閱

I took out a *subscription* to Reader's Digest for two years. (87 中原，86 成大)

summary ﹝ 'sʌmərɪ ﹞ *n.* 摘要

He didn't have time to read the whole book; he just read a *summary*. (87 政大，80 輔大)

supervision ﹝ ˌsupɚ'vɪʒən ﹞ *n.* 監督

The man finished his report under the *supervision* of his manager. (85 交大，80 淡江)

super	+	vis	+	ion
above	+	*see*	+	*n.*

surgeon 〔ˈsɝdʒən〕 n. 外科醫生

A *surgeon* operates on sick people.

（88 銘傳，83 中興）

surplus 〔ˈsɝplʌs〕 n. 剩餘

The store has a *surplus* of canned peaches, so it put them on sale.

（87 政大）

sur	+ plus
|	|
above	+ *more*

surroundings 〔səˈraʊndɪŋz〕 n. pl. 環境

The girl realized she was lost when she did not recognize her *surroundings*.

（86 輔大、銘傳）

survey 〔ˈsɝve〕 n. 調查

The company conducted a *survey* to find out what people thought of its products.

（86 中原）

sur	+ vey
|	|
over	+ *see*

suspicion 〔 sə'spɪʃən 〕 n. 懷疑

The shopkeeper looked at me with *suspicion*, but I would never think of trying to steal anything. (87 台北大，84 淡江)

sus	+ pic	+ ion
under	+ *see*	+ *n.*

symbol 〔'sɪmbḷ 〕 n. 象徵

A heart shape is the *symbol* of love.

(86 成大，85 逢甲)

symmetry 〔'sɪmɪtrɪ 〕 n. 對稱

The chairs were arranged with perfect *symmetry* — five on each side of the room.

(86 成大)

sym	+ metry
same	+ *measure*（測量）

sympathy 〔'sɪmpəθɪ〕 *n.* 同情

Bob received many cards and letters from friends who wanted to offer their *sympathy*.

（85 逢甲，81 淡江）

> sym + pathy
> | |
> *same + feelings*

symphony 〔'sɪmfənɪ〕 *n.* 交響樂

The orchestra played one of Beethoven's *symphonies* last night. （86 成大）

symptom 〔'sɪmptəm〕 *n.* 症狀

Headaches and fever are both *symptoms* of illness. （87 中原，86 成大、逢甲）

syndrome 〔'sɪn͵drom〕 *n.* 徵候群

Several patients suffering from the same *syndrome* have come to the hospital this week. （86 逢甲）

synonym 〔'sɪnə,nɪm 〕 *n.* 同義字

Instead of writing the same word again, why don't you use a *synonym*?

（86 成大、逢甲）

syn	+ onym
same	+ *name*

T t

taboo 〔 tə'bu 〕 *n.* 禁忌

In some societies, using a dead person's name is a *taboo*. （84 台北大）

target 〔'tɑrgɪt 〕 *n.* 目標

I shot the arrow at the *target*, but I missed it.

（86 中興、逢甲）

temptation 〔 tɛmp'teʃən 〕 *n.* 誘惑

The child couldn't resist the *temptation* of the candy and ate all of it.

（80 中興）

tempt	+ ation
try	+ *n.*

tenant (ˈtɛnənt) *n.* 房客

Do you own your house or are you a
tenant? (82淡江)

```
ten  + ant
 |      |
hold +  人
```

tendency (ˈtɛndənsɪ) *n.* 傾向

Many doctors are still general practitioners,
but the *tendency* is toward specialization in
medicine. (85文化,83清大)

tension (ˈtɛnʃən) *n.* 緊張

Mental patients are sometimes given drugs
to reduce *tension*. (85交大)

territory (ˈtɛrəˌtorɪ) *n.* 領土

Some animals will defend their *territory* by
fighting anyone that enters it.

(86清大)

```
terri + tory
  |      |
earth + place
```

Check List

( ) 1. stroll

( ) 2. summary

( ) 3. surroundings

( ) 4. survey

( ) 5. suspicion

( ) 6. symbol

( ) 7. symmetry

( ) 8. sympathy

( ) 9. taboo

( ) 10. target

( ) 11. temptation

( ) 12. tenant

( ) 13. tendency

( ) 14. tension

( ) 15. territory

A. lure

B. anxiety

C. environment

D. lodger

E. walk

F. sign ; emblem

G. digest

H. balance

I. aim ; goal

J. inquiry

K. prohibition

L. trend

M. indication

N. domain

O. disbelief

Vocabulary Ratings

5–7 *Good*   8–11 *Very Good*   12–15 *Excellent*

·Synonyms·

1. stroll
= walk

2. summary
= digest

3. surroundings
= environment

4. survey
= inquiry

5. suspicion
= disbelief
= doubt

6. symbol
= sign
= emblem

7. symmetry
= balance

8. symptom
= indication

9. taboo
= prohibition

10. target
= aim = goal

11. temptation
= lure

12. tenant
= lodger
= boarder

13. tendency
= trend
= inclination

14. tension
= anxiety
= nervousness

15. territory
= domain
= land

theme 〔 θim 〕 *n.* 主題

Love has been a recurrent *theme* in literature.

（87 中興）

therapy 〔'θɛrəpɪ 〕 *n.* 治療法

Rest is good *therapy* for a cold. （86 輔大）

thermometer 〔 θə'mɑmətɚ 〕 *n.* 溫度計

The nurse took the child's temperature with

a *thermometer*. （86 淡江）

thermo	+	meter
heat	+	*measure*

thorn 〔 θɔrn 〕 *n.* 刺

There is no rose without a *thorn*. （87 成大）

timber 〔'tɪmbɚ 〕 *n.* 木材

Laurels are valued for their aromatic oils,

spices, edible fruits and *timber*. （86 中原）

timetable 〔'taɪm,tebḷ〕 *n.* 時間表

The governor will set a *timetable* for the appointment of his subordinates. （86 中興）

torrent 〔'tɔrənt〕 *n.* 急流

After the heavy rain, the stream became a *torrent*. （87 中正）

transit 〔'trænsɪt〕 *n.* 運輸

The package is in *transit*. It left New York on Monday and is expected to arrive here tomorrow. （85 逢甲）

trans + it
| |
across + go

transition 〔træn'zɪʃən〕 *n.* 過渡期

The country has gone through a *transition* from an agricultural society to an industrial one. （86 清大）

transmission 〔 træns'mɪʃən 〕 *n.* 傳送

With a computer, the *transmission* of
images takes only seconds. (85 淡江)

```
trans  + miss + ion
  |        |      |
across  + send  +  n.
```

tremor 〔'trɛmɚ 〕 *n.* 震動

Before the earthquake hit the area, many
minor *tremors* were felt. (83 淡江)

triumph 〔'traɪəmf 〕 *n.* 勝利

The baseball team is celebrating its *triumph*
with a big party tonight. (87 清大)

turmoil 〔't3mɔɪl 〕 *n.* 混亂

The political *turmoil* in that nation forced
many people to leave their homes.

(86 成大,81 交大)

U u

unemployment 〔ˌʌnɪmˈplɔɪmənt 〕

n. 失業

During the recession, the *unemployment* rate reached a new high. (85 逢甲，83 交大)

uproar 〔ˈʌpˌror 〕 *n.* 騷動

The demonstration ended in an *uproar*.

(83 輔大)

V v

variety 〔 vəˈraɪətɪ 〕 *n.* 種類

It is important to eat a *variety* of foods to get enough nutrition. (86 逢甲，81 交大)

vegetarian 〔ˌvɛdʒəˈtɛrɪən 〕 *n.* 素食者

She is a *vegetarian*, and is very careful about what she eats. (81 逢甲)

vehicle 〔'viɪkḷ 〕 *n.* 車輛

The school does not allow anyone to park a *vehicle* in front of the entrance. (86 輔大)

vehi	+	cle
carry	+	物

ventilation 〔 ˌvɛntḷ'eʃən 〕 *n.* 通風

There is good *ventilation* in this room because of the two large windows. (86 私醫)

venti	+	lat(e)	+	ion
wind	+	bring	+	n.

verge 〔 vɝdʒ 〕 *n.* 邊緣

Due to the recession, the company was on the *verge* of bankruptcy. (88 輔大)

version 〔'vɝʒən 〕 *n.* 版本

In many respects the new *version* is not as good as the old one. (85 文化，83 私醫)

violation 〔͵vaɪəˈleʃən〕 *n.* 違反

Turning left here is a *violation* of the traffic regulations. You could get a ticket. (86 私醫)

virtue 〔ˈvɝtʃʊ〕 *n.* 美德

Humility and diligence are traditional Chinese *virtues*. (86 政大)

vogue 〔vog〕 *n.* 流行

Clothing made of denim is in *vogue* this year. (85 中興)

voyage 〔ˈvɔɪ·ɪdʒ〕 *n.* 旅行

My parents took a *voyage* on a luxury cruise ship to celebrate their anniversary.

(89 成大，81 台大)

```
voy + age
 |      |
way  +  n.
```

•Check List•

(   ) 1. theme   A. schedule

(   ) 2. thorn   B. disobedience

(   ) 3. timber   C. vibration

(   ) 4. timetable   D. fashion

(   ) 5. torrent   E. journey

(   ) 6. transmission   F. lumber

(   ) 7. tremor   G. prickle

(   ) 8. triumph   H. victory

(   ) 9. turmoil   I. goodness

(   ) 10. unemployment   J. joblessness

(   ) 11. version   K. chaos

(   ) 12. violation   L. conduction

(   ) 13. virtue   M. outpouring

(   ) 14. vogue   N. account

(   ) 15. voyage   O. subject

| Vocabulary Ratings |

5–7 *Good*   8–11 *Very Good*   12–15 *Excellent*

Synonyms

1. theme
   = subject
   = topic

2. thorn
   = prickle

3. timber
   = lumber
   = wood

4. timetable
   = schedule

5. torrent
   = outpouring

6. transmission
   = conduction

7. tremor
   = tremble
   = vibration
   = quake

8. triumph
   = victory

9. turmoil
   = chaos
   = disorder

10. unemployment
    = joblessness

11. version
    = account

12. violation
    = disobedience

13. virtue
    = goodness

14. vogue
    = fashion

15. voyage
    = journey

動　詞

abide 〔 ə'baɪd 〕 v. 遵守

When you enter the room, you should *abide*
by the rules here. (81 台大)

abolish 〔 ə'bɑlɪʃ 〕 v. 廢除

The president decided to *abolish* the
unreasonable rules. (85 輔大)

abridge 〔 ə'brɪdʒ 〕 v. 縮短

The book is too difficult for students, so it
will be *abridged* to suit their needs.

(84 交大，82 文化)

```
a  + bridge
|        |
to + short
```

absorb 〔 əb'sɔrb 〕 v. 吸收

It is important for everyone to *absorb*
knowledge wherever possible. (85 銘傳，80 文化)

abuse 〔 ə'bjuz 〕 *v.* 虐待

To *abuse* an animal or a child is not humane.

（81 台大，80 文化）

accelerate 〔 æk'sɛlə,ret 〕 *v.* 加速

We have to *accelerate* industrial
development in our country. （83 文化）

ac + celer	+ ate
| |	|
to + *swift* (快速的) +	*v.*

accommodate 〔 ə'kɑmə,det 〕 *v.* 容納

The stadium can *accommodate* more than
5000 people. （84 淡江）

accomplish 〔 ə'kɑmplɪʃ 〕 *v.* 達成

Stick with me and you'll *accomplish* your
goal. （81 台大）

accumulate 〔 ə'kjumjə‚let 〕 v. 累積

He *accumulated* a huge collection of stamps in his school life. (86 逢甲，85 銘傳)

```
ac + cumulate
 |      |
to + heap up （堆積）
```

acknowledge 〔 ək'nɑlɪdʒ 〕 v. 承認

It is *acknowledged* that the pen is mightier than the sword. (86 中興，84 淡江)

acquire 〔 ə'kwaɪr 〕 v. 獲得

Study hard, and you will *acquire* knowledge little by little. (81 台大)

```
ac + quire
 |     |
to + seek
```

adapt 〔 ə'dæpt 〕 v. 使適應

At the meeting, the club made an effort to *adapt* the constitution to the needs of the occasion.

(82 成大，81 台大、淡江)

```
ad + apt
 |    |
to + fit
```

address ﹝ ə'drɛs ﹞ v. 提出

The purpose of the conference is to *address* the major issues that have been plaguing the institution. (85 台大)

adhere ﹝ əd'hɪr ﹞ v. 堅持

You should *adhere* to your goal and try hard to achieve it. (84 淡江)

adjust ﹝ ə'dʒʌst ﹞ v. 調整

She *adjusted* her seat cushion to a more comfortable position. (86 成大)

```
ad + just
 |     |
to + right
```

admire ﹝ əd'maɪr ﹞ v. 讚賞

His works of art have been greatly *admired* by many people. (87 政大)

admit ﹝ əd'mɪt ﹞ v. 承認

I have to *admit* that I have made some mistakes in dealing with the matter. (85 東吳)

adopt 〔 ə'dɑpt 〕 v. 採用

After careful thinking, we decided to *adopt* the new method.

（86 逢甲，81 台大）

```
ad  +  opt
 |      |
to  +  wish
```

adore 〔 ə'dor 〕 v. 喜愛

The newborn baby was *adored* by all the family members. （81 台大）

advocate 〔'ædvəˌket 〕 v. 提倡

He has tirelessly been *advocating* the rights of workers for years.

（88 中央，85 銘傳）

```
ad  +  voc  +  ate
 |      |      |
to  +  call  +  v.
```

affect 〔 ə'fɛkt 〕 v. 影響

The weather often *affects* our moods; we feel upset on a rainy day and cheerful on a sunny day. （88 中正，86 交大，84 東吳）

aggravate 〔'ægrə‚vet 〕 v. 惡化

The situation of the poor was *aggravated*
by the tax increase. (89 成大, 86 逢甲)

ag + grav + ate
│ │ │
to + *heavy* + *v.*

alert 〔 ə'lɜt 〕 v. 警告

I *alerted* the captain to the presence of an
unidentified craft that was approaching.

(86 輔大)

alleviate 〔 ə'livɪ‚et 〕 v. 減輕

The drugs could only *alleviate* the pain, not
provide the cure. (82 中興, 81 交大, 80 淡江)

alter 〔'ɔltə 〕 v. 改變

The plan was *altered*; we had to delay our
departure time. (86 逢甲, 85 銘傳, 81 清大)

Check List

( ) 1. abide	A. adjust
( ) 2. abridge	B. maltreat
( ) 3. abuse	C. acknowledge
( ) 4. accelerate	D. influence
( ) 5. accomplish	E. change
( ) 6. acquire	F. relieve
( ) 7. adapt	G. comply
( ) 8. address	H. forward
( ) 9. adhere	I. achieve
( )10. admit	J. worsen
( )11. advocate	K. shorten
( )12. affect	L. obtain
( )13. aggravate	M. promote
( )14. alleviate	N. stick
( )15. alter	O. hasten

Vocabulary Ratings

5–7 *Good*   8–11 *Very Good*   12–15 *Excellent*

·Synonyms·

1. abide
   = comply

2. abridge
   = shorten

3. abuse
   = maltreat
   = misuse

4. accelerate
   = hasten
   = speed up

5. accomplish
   = achieve
   = attain

6. affect
   = influence

7. adapt
   = adjust
   = accustom

8. address
   = forward

9. adhere
   = stick = cling

10. admit
    = acknowledge
    = confess

11. advocate
    = promote

12. acquire
    = obtain = get

13. aggravate
    = worsen

14. alleviate
    = relieve = ease

15. alter
    = change

announce 〔 ə'naʊns 〕 v. 宣布

The teacher *announced* that the final exam
would be held in May.

(88 中正，87 政大，83 中興)

```
an  +  nounce
 |        |
to  +  report
```

annoy 〔 ə'nɔɪ 〕 v. 使苦惱

He was greatly *annoyed* by the new and
unexpected development. (81 淡江)

anticipate 〔 æn'tɪsə,pet 〕 v. 預期

A good leader can *anticipate* people's
responses. (86 銘傳)

appeal 〔 ə'pil 〕 v. 吸引

Bright colors or moving objects *appeal* to
little babies. (89 輔大，87 中原，81 台大)

applaud 〔 ə'plɔd 〕 v. 鼓掌

When the concert was over,
the audience *applauded*
enthusiastically. (85 靜宜)

```
ap  +  plaud
 |       |
to  +  clap
```

arise 〔 ə'raɪz 〕 v. 產生

It is impossible for life to *arise* on Venus because of its intense surface heat.

（90、85 台大，85 文化）

arouse 〔 ə'raʊz 〕 v. 激起

The anonymous phone call *aroused* his interest. （90 台大，85 文化）

arrest 〔 ə'rɛst 〕 v. 逮捕

The man was *arrested* for drunken driving.

（87 逢甲，82 台大）

ascribe 〔 ə'skraɪb 〕 v. 歸因於

She *ascribed* her failure to poor health.

（83 政大）

assault 〔 ə'sɔlt 〕 v. 攻擊

The city was *assaulted* by our enemies.

（81 台大）

assemble 〔 əˈsɛmbl̩ 〕 *v.* 集合

The students *assembled* their notes from the whole semester before beginning their study session for the final exam.

（86、84 私醫）

as + semble
to + same

assess 〔 əˈsɛs 〕 *v.* 評估

It is difficult to *assess* the effects of the new law as it has only been in effect for two months. （88 銘傳）

assist 〔 əˈsɪst 〕 *v.* 幫助

She hired a maid to *assist* her in keeping house. （81 台大）

associate 〔 əˈsoʃɪˌet 〕 *v.* 聯想

People always *associate* the color red with love and passion. （81 台大）

assume 〔ə'sjum〕 *v.* 認爲

Never *assume* you have learned enough.
Knowledge is limitless.

（87中興，81台大）

```
as  + sume
 |      |
to  + take
```

assure 〔ə'ʃur〕 *v.* 保證

He *assured* me that we would make it in
this way. （81中興）

astonish 〔ə'stɑnɪʃ〕 *v.* 使驚訝

We were *astonished* by the number of the
complaints. （83文化，81淡江，80清大）

attain 〔ə'ten〕 *v.* 達到

He *attained* recognition for his hard work.

（88台大，85輔大）

```
at  +   tain
 |       |
to  + hold , keep
```

attribute 〔 əˋtrɪbjut 〕 v. 歸因於

Her bad performance was *attributed* to stage fright. (88 中正、銘傳，84 政大，81 台大)

B b

ban 〔 bæn 〕 v. 禁止

The sale of the drug will be *banned* on August 1. (85 中興)

behave 〔 bɪˋhev 〕 v. 行為

Mary has been *behaving* in a very strange manner lately. (82 清大)

benefit 〔 ˋbɛnəfɪt 〕 v. 獲益

I can see the advantages in this for you, but how will I *benefit*?

(88 政大，85 銘傳，82 政大)

bene + fit
| |
good + do

bewilder 〔 bɪ'wɪldə 〕 v. 使困惑

His unusual behavior *bewildered* us all.

（86 中正，85 文化）

boast 〔 bost 〕 v. 自誇

We have been listening to Ernie *boasting* about what he did last night for an hour.

（83 輔大）

C c

calculate 〔'kælkjə‚let 〕 v. 計算

The ancient Chinese used abacuses to *calculate*. （84 文化）

capture 〔'kæptʃə 〕 v. 捕捉

They went hunting and *captured* a fox.

（80 淡江）

·Check List·

(   ) 1. announce   A. gather

(   ) 2. appeal   B. suppose

(   ) 3. arouse   C. ascribe

(   ) 4. assault   D. seize

(   ) 5. assemble   E. puzzle

(   ) 6. assess   F. declare

(   ) 7. assist   G. forbid

(   ) 8. associate   H. amaze

(   ) 9. assume   I. attack

(   ) 10. astonish   J. help ; aid

(   ) 11. attribute   K. attract

(   ) 12. ban   L. brag ; show off

(   ) 13. bewilder   M. evaluate

(   ) 14. boast   N. connect

(   ) 15. capture   O. stimulate

Vocabulary Ratings

5–7 *Good*   8–11 *Very Good*   12–15 *Excellent*

·Synonyms·

1. announce
   = declare

2. appeal
   = attract

3. arouse
   = stimulate
   = excite

4. assault
   = attack

5. assemble
   = gather

6. assess
   = evaluate

7. assist
   = help = aid

8. associate
   = connect
   = relate

9. assume
   = suppose
   = presume

10. astonish
    = amaze
    = surprise

11. attribute
    = ascribe

12. ban
    = forbid
    = prohibit

13. bewilder
    = puzzle
    = confuse

14. boast = brag
    = show off

15. capture
    = seize

characterize 〔'kærɪktə,raɪz 〕 *v.*

以~爲特色

The education system here is *characterized* by an emphasis on success in exams. (82 政大)

circulate 〔'sɝkjə,let 〕 *v.* 循環

Drinking makes blood *circulate* more quickly. (87 中興，86 輔大，85 清大、私醫，82 文化)

circul + ate
| |
ring (環) + *v.*

clar + ify
| |
clear + *v.*

clarify 〔'klærə,faɪ 〕 *v.* 澄清

Your remark is really perplexing. Would you please *clarify* your statement?

(87、81 台大，82 中興)

classify 〔'klæsə,faɪ 〕 *v.* 分類

Books are *classified* by subject in the library.

(89 輔大，88 政大，81 台大)

collapse 〔 kəˈlæps 〕 *v.* 崩塌

Several bridges *collapsed* due to the severe earthquake. (82 台大)

col	+ lapse
together	+ *slip*（滑）

commit 〔 kəˈmɪt 〕 *v.* 犯（罪）

He has no criminal record; that is, he has never *committed* a crime. (86 逢甲)

compensate 〔ˈkɑmpənˌset 〕 *v.* 賠償

Many factories *compensate* their workers if they are hurt at work. (86 清大，84 淡江)

compete 〔 kəmˈpit 〕 *v.* 競爭

There are a total of 30 persons *competing* for the championship.

(86 中原)

com	+ pete
together	+ *seek*

comply ﹝kəm'plaɪ﹞ *v.* 遵守

The new members *complied* with the club's regulations. (89 輔大，82 台大)

compose ﹝kəm'poz﹞ *v.* 組成

Water is *composed* of hydrogen and oxygen.

(89 成大，85 逢甲)

```
com + pose
 |      |
all  +  put
```

compromise ﹝'kamprə,maɪz﹞ *v.* 妥協

Mr. Pitt refused to *compromise* with them on the matter. (86 成大)

conceal ﹝kən'sil﹞ *v.* 隱藏

No one knows what he's thinking. He always *conceals* his feelings.

(88 銘傳，85 清大，81 淡江)

concede 〔 kən'sid 〕 v. 承認

He *conceded* the fact that he was wrong.

（80 輔大）

con	+ cede
together +	go

conceive 〔 kən'siv 〕 v. 想像

In the 19th century, the idea that anyone would walk on the moon had not even been *conceived*. （83 交大）

conclude 〔 kən'klud 〕 v. 下結論

The police *concluded* that he couldn't have possibly committed the crime. （90 台大，86 私醫）

condemn 〔 kən'dɛm 〕 v. 譴責

Their violent action was *condemned* by the public. （88 中央）

condense 〔 kən'dɛns 〕 v. 濃縮

Your essay was too long. Please *condense* it to 300 words. (84 交大)

```
con + dense
 |      |
all +  濃密
```

```
con + fess
 |      |
all + speak
```

confess 〔 kən'fɛs 〕 v. 承認

Manson *confessed* that he had committed the crime. (87 中興，85 清大)

confide 〔 kən'faɪd 〕 v. 透露（秘密）

If you *confide* a secret to someone, you tell him about it and trust him not to tell anyone else. (86 銘傳)

confine 〔 kən'faɪn 〕 v. 限制

The man was *confined* to a mental institution for three years. (83 文化)

confirm〔kənˊfɝm〕v. 證實

Smith's testimony served to *confirm* that of the previous witness.

（82清大，81台大）

```
con + firm
 |     |
all + 堅固的
```

confiscate〔ˊkɑnfɪsˌket〕v. 沒收

The teacher *confiscated* his cell phone after asking him to turn it off three times. （85台大）

confront〔kənˊfrʌnt〕v. 面對

Now a big problem *confronts* us, leaving us in a dilemma.

（85中興）

```
con    + front
 |        |
together + 前面
```

confuse〔kənˊfjuz〕v. 使混淆

We were really *confused* as to who was actually responsible. （86中興）

·Check List·

(   ) 1. classify   A. offend

(   ) 2. commit   B. obey

(   ) 3. compensate   C. compress

(   ) 4. compete   D. admit

(   ) 5. comply   E. restrict

(   ) 6. compose   F. categorize

(   ) 7. conceal   G. encounter

(   ) 8. concede   H. denounce

(   ) 9. conceive   I. hide ; cover

(   ) 10. condemn   J. make up for

(   ) 11. condense   K. prove

(   ) 12. confine   L. imagine

(   ) 13. confirm   M. comprise

(   ) 14. confront   N. baffle

(   ) 15. confuse   O. contest

Vocabulary Ratings

5–7 *Good*   8–11 *Very Good*   12–15 *Excellent*

Synonyms

1. classify
   = categorize

2. commit
   = offend

3. compensate
   = make up for

4. compete
   = contest

5. comply
   = abide
   = obey
   = observe

6. confront
   = encounter
   = face

7. concede
   = admit
   = confess

8. conceive
   = imagine

9. condemn
   = denounce
   = reproach

10. condense
    = compress

11. confine
    = restrict
    = limit

12. confirm
    = prove

13. compose
    = comprise

14. conceal
    = hide = cover

15. confuse
    = baffle

consent 〔kənˈsɛnt〕 v. 同意

Her parents didn't *consent* to her marrying that penniless man. (85文化,82台大)

consist 〔kənˈsɪst〕 v. 組成

The book *consists* mainly of photographs; it doesn't appeal to me. (88中正,85逢甲)

console 〔kənˈsol〕 v. 安慰

Helen was so sad about the bad news that I didn't know how to *console* her. (84成大)

con + sole	con + sume
together + alone	all + take

consume 〔kənˈsum〕 v. 消耗

His old car *consumed* a lot of gas, so he decided to buy a new one. (81逢甲)

contract 〔 kən'trækt 〕 *v.* 收縮

Metal expands and *contracts* according to the change of temperature.

（86 私醫，83 中興）

contribute 〔 kən'trɪbjʊt 〕 *v.* 貢獻

Women *contribute* no less to the society than men. （90、81 台大，90 輔大）

converse 〔 kən'vɝs 〕 *v.* 談話

Conversing with foreigners in English seems difficult to many people. （81 中興）

convert 〔 kən'vɝt 〕 *v.* 改變

The gymnasium of the school has been *converted* to a shelter for victims of the flood. （85 台大）

correct 〔 kə'rɛkt 〕 *v.* 更正

He wants to *correct* his mistake before it
is too late.

（86 中正，85 清大）

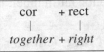

cor	+ rect
|	|
together	+ *right*

crave 〔 krɛv 〕 *v.* 渴望

Sometimes, while living in a foreign country,
one *craves* a special dish from home. （85 銘傳）

crush 〔 krʌʃ 〕 *v.* 壓碎

The toy dropped on the street was *crushed*
under the wheels of the car. （86 銘傳）

D d

debate 〔 dɪ'bet 〕 *v.* 辯論

It has often been *debated* whether students
should wear uniforms or not.

（88 政大，86 成大、輔大、私醫，81 淡江）

deceive 〔dɪ'siv〕 v. 欺騙

The policeman was *deceived* by the boy's innocent manner. (83 淡江)

declare 〔dɪ'klɛr〕 v. 宣布

India *declared* independence from the UK in 1948. (91、81 台大)

decline 〔dɪ'klaɪn〕 v. 婉拒

He *declined* the offer of a high reward with courtesy.

(84 交大，81 台大、淡江)

```
de  + cline
 |      |
down + bend (彎曲)
```

defeat 〔dɪ'fit〕 v. 擊敗

He tried every way to *defeat* his opponent.

(86 逢甲，84 成大)

demand 〔dɪ'mænd〕 v. 要求

He *demanded* she give him the keys to his motorcycle back, but she refused. (86 中興)

demolish〔dɪˋmɑlɪʃ〕v. 破壞

The government *demolished* the illegal houses despite public protest. (86 私醫，85 中興)

demonstrate〔ˋdɛmən͵stret〕v. 示範

The salesman *demonstrated* how to operate the new washing machine.

(86 清大，83 文化，80 中興)

```
de  + monstr + ate
 |      |        |
fully + show  + v.
```

denounce〔dɪˋnaʊns〕v. 譴責

She *denounced* the media's treatment of her as unjust.

(85 中興)

```
de   + nounce
 |       |
down + report
```

depart〔dɪˋpɑrt〕v. 離開

Before *departing*, Lawrence shook hands with all his old colleagues. (81 清大)

depress〔 dɪˈprɛs 〕 v. 使沮喪

The news of his ex-wife's remarriage *depressed* him even further. (87中原，85文化)

deprive 〔 dɪˈpraɪv 〕 v. 剝奪

Sentenced to death, the man was *deprived* of all his civil rights. (80中興)

derive 〔 dəˈraɪv 〕 v. 起源於

Some English words are *derived* from Latin and Greek. (87、80中興)

descend 〔 dɪˈsɛnd 〕 v. 下降

She *descended* the long flight of stairs carefully. (85私醫)

de	+ scend
down	+ climb

Check List

( ) 1. consist   A. rectify

( ) 2. console   B. dispute

( ) 3. contract   C. destroy

( ) 4. correct   D. reject

( ) 5. crave   E. originate

( ) 6. crush   F. contain

( ) 7. debate   G. dishearten

( ) 8. deceive   H. command

( ) 9. decline   I. comfort

( ) 10. defeat   J. cheat

( ) 11. demand   K. squeeze

( ) 12. demolish   L. condemn

( ) 13. denounce   M. shrink

( ) 14. depress   N. beat

( ) 15. derive   O. desire

Vocabulary Ratings

5–7 *Good*   8–11 *Very Good*   12–15 *Excellent*

·Synonyms·

1. consist
   = contain

2. console
   = comfort

3. contract
   = shrink
   = diminish

4. correct
   = rectify

5. crave
   = desire
   = long for

6. demolish
   = destroy
   = tear down

7. debate
   = dispute
   = argue

8. deceive
   = cheat
   = take in

9. decline
   = reject

10. defeat
    = beat

11. demand
    = command

12. crush
    = squeeze

13. denounce
    = condemn

14. depress
    = dishearten
    = sadden

15. derive
    = originate

designate ﹝'dɛzɪg,net﹞ v. 指定

The old building was *designated* as a historic monument recently by the Ministry of the Interior.

（86、85 銘傳）

de	+ sign +	ate
|	|	|
down	+ *mark* +	*v.*

despise ﹝dɪ'spaɪz﹞ v. 輕視

After they became slightly better off, they *despised* us as poor relations. （86 交大）

detect ﹝dɪ'tɛkt﹞ v. 偵測

Security officials say that computer crime is easy to accomplish and hard to *detect*.

（86 中原，84 私醫，82 台大）

deter ﹝dɪ'tɝ﹞ v. 阻礙

The bad weather did not *deter* us from going for a walk. （86 私醫，81 清大）

devote 〔 dɪ'vot 〕 v. 奉獻

Mother Teresa *devoted* all her life to helping poor people. （90 輔大，85 文化）

diagnose 〔 ˌdaɪəg'noz 〕 v. 診斷

A technological development increased the accuracy in *diagnosing* a disease.

（86 成大，83 交大）

diminish 〔 də'mɪnɪʃ 〕 v. 減少

If we create a society in which injustice is not tolerated, incidents of murder will *diminish*. （86 銘傳、私醫，83 淡江）

di	+	min	+	ish
apart	+	*small*	+	*v.*

discard 〔 dɪs'kɑrd 〕 v. 丟棄

These old newspapers are useless. Let's *discard* them. （84、81 交大，80 文化）

disclose 〔 dɪs'kloz 〕 v. 揭發

His secret has been *disclosed* by the
magazine. (86 私醫)

```
dis  +  close
 |        |
not  +  close
```

discourage 〔 dɪs'kɝɪdʒ 〕 v. 使氣餒

A series of failures *discouraged* him. He
gave up in despair. (81 台大)

dismiss 〔 dɪs'mɪs 〕 v. 解散

The teacher *dismissed* the class when the
bell rang. (85 台大,85 逢甲,82 文化)

dispel 〔 dɪ'spɛl 〕 v. 驅散

The riot police used tear gas to *dispel* the
mob who gathered in the square.

(淡江)

```
dis  +  pel
 |       |
away  +  drive (趕)
```

dissolve 〔 dɪˈzɑlv 〕 v. 溶解

She stirred the coffee to make the sugar cube
dissolve faster.

（86中正，85台大）

dis	+	solve
apart	+	loosen（放鬆）

distinguish 〔 dɪˈstɪŋgwɪʃ 〕 v. 區分

I can't *distinguish* one twin from the other.

（87台大、逢甲，85中正、淡江）

distract 〔 dɪˈstrækt 〕 v. 分心

The noise outside *distracted* him from his
study. （80淡江）

dis	+	tract
away	+	draw（拉）

distribute 〔 dɪˈstrɪbjut 〕 v. 分發

The professor *distributed* exam papers to
all the students in the classroom.

（85文化，81台大）

disturb 〔 dɪ'stɝb 〕 v. 打擾

Sorry to *disturb* you, but I need to ask you an important question. (85 台大、銘傳、文化)

drown 〔 draʊn 〕 v. 淹死

I almost *drowned*; luckily, Henry pulled me out of the water to safety. (85 台大)

E e

elaborate 〔 ɪ'læbə‚ret 〕 v. 詳述

Could you please *elaborate* your ideas about this issue?

(86 中正、銘傳)

e	+ labor	+ ate
|	|	|
out	+ *work*	+ *v.*

elevate 〔 'ɛlə‚vet 〕 v. 提高

Our government has been working hard to *elevate* people's living standards. (85 中興)

eliminate 〔 ɪ'lɪmə,net 〕 v. 消除

They worked hard to *eliminate* any unnecessary conflict within the organization.

（86 成大，85 中興）

```
e  + limin + ate
|      |      |
out + limit +  v.
```

embrace 〔 ɪm'bres 〕 v. 擁抱

Upon seeing her son after a long separation, the mother *embraced* him tightly. （82 交大）

emerge 〔 ɪ'mɜdʒ 〕 v. 出現

The sun soon *emerged* from behind the clouds. （88 銘傳）

```
e  + merge
|     |
out + sink（沈）
```

```
e  + migr + ate
|     |      |
out + move +  v.
```

emigrate 〔 'ɛmə,gret 〕 v. 移出

The Wangs decided to *emigrate* from Taiwan to the United States. （86 中原）

•Check List•

( ) 1. designate
( ) 2. despise
( ) 3. detect
( ) 4. deter
( ) 5. devote

( ) 6. disclose
( ) 7. discourage
( ) 8. dispel
( ) 9. dissolve
( ) 10. distract

( ) 11. disturb
( ) 12. elevate
( ) 13. eliminate
( ) 14. embrace
( ) 15. emerge

A. appoint
B. appear
C. raise ; lift
D. melt
E. reveal

F. perceive
G. disperse
H. dedicate
I. remove
J. hug

K. prevent
L. divert
M. dispirit
N. interrupt
O. scorn

Vocabulary Ratings

5–7 *Good*   8–11 *Very Good*   12–15 *Excellent*

Synonyms

1. designate
   = appoint

2. despise
   = scorn

3. detect
   = perceive
   = notice

4. deter
   = prevent

5. eliminate
   = remove
   = get rid of

6. disclose
   = reveal
   = unveil

7. discourage
   = dispirit
   = dishearten

8. dispel
   = disperse

9. dissolve
   = melt

10. distract
    = divert

11. disturb
    = interrupt
    = disrupt

12. elevate
    = raise = lift

13. devote
    = dedicate

14. embrace
    = hug

15. emerge
    = appear
    = arise

emphasize 〔'ɛmfə,saɪz 〕 v. 強調

The conference *emphasized* the importance of the microchip industry. (85 銘傳，84 政大)

enchant 〔 ɪn'tʃænt 〕 v. 使著迷

She was *enchanted* by the flowers you sent her. (83 中興)

enclose 〔 ɪn'kloz 〕 v. 附寄

I *enclosed* a photo of myself in the first letter to my new pen pal.

(86 輔大)

```
en + close
 |      |
in + close
```

encounter 〔 ɪn'kaʊntə 〕 v. 遭遇

The travelers *encountered* many tough problems but finally solved them. (84 輔大)

endanger 〔 ɪn'dendʒɚ 〕 v. 危害

You may *endanger* your career by making such a stupid decision. (87輔大)

endure 〔 ɪn'djur 〕 v. 忍受

I have *endured* your unfair treatment for too long. I want out. (87成大)

enforce 〔 ɪn'fors 〕 v. 執行

The police are making every effort to *enforce* the new law. (86交大)

enhance 〔 ɪn'hæns 〕 v. 提高

Charm can *enhance* beauty and attraction in women. (86銘傳，82、80淡江，81中興)

```
en + hance
 |      |
in  +  high
```

enlarge 〔 ɪn'lɑrdʒ 〕 v. 放大

This photo is beautiful. Let's have it *enlarged*. (91、82台大)

enlighten 〔 ɪn'laɪtn̩ 〕 v. 啓發

My trip to Italy has really *enlightened* me as to the true meaning of art. (81 淡江)

entertain 〔 ˌɛntɚ'ten 〕 v. 使娛樂

The host *entertained* all the guests with his funny tricks. (90 輔大，82 交大)

entitle 〔 ɪn'taɪtl̩ 〕 v. 有資格

She is *entitled* to whatever success she can get. (83 中央)

equivocate 〔 ɪ'kwɪvəˌket 〕 v. 用字含糊

Lawyers are often accused of *equivocating*.

(81 淡江)

equi	+ voc	+ ate
together	+ voice	+ v.

eradicate 〔 ɪ'rædɪˌket 〕 v. 消滅

It was a decisive victory for medicine
when the disease of smallpox was finally
eradicated.

（84 交大，83 淡江）

e	+ radi	+ ate
|	|	|
out	+ *root*	+ *v.*

erase 〔 ɪ'res 〕 v. 擦掉

Someone has *erased* part of the address on
this letter. （83 淡江）

estimate 〔'ɛstəˌmet 〕 v. 估計

The archaeologist *estimated* that the artifacts
found in the ruins were 2000 years old.

（85 中興）

evade 〔 ɪ'ved 〕 v. 閃避

He tried to *evade* her question, but she
wouldn't let him escape so easily. （86 私醫）

evaporate 〔 ɪˈvæpəˌret 〕 *v.* 蒸發

Water *evaporates* when it is boiled.

（86 私醫）

e	+ vapor + ate
out	+ 蒸氣 + *v.*

examine 〔 ɪgˈzæmɪn 〕 *v.* 檢查

The doctor *examined* the patient's back and made a diagnosis. （86 中興）

exceed 〔 ɪkˈsid 〕 *v.* 超過

When supply *exceeds* demand, the price will go down. （86 中興）

ex	+ ceed
out	+ *go*

exert 〔 ɪgˈzɜt 〕 *v.* 努力

We must *exert* ourselves in order to give in return as much as we have received.

（87 文化）

exhale 〔 ɛks'hel 〕 v. 呼氣

Every time he *exhaled* his
chest hurt. (85 政大)

ex	+	hale
out	+	*breathe*

exhibit 〔 ɪg'zɪbɪt 〕 v. 展示

They *exhibited* great power of endurance
during the climb. (84 文化)

expand 〔 ɪk'spænd 〕 v. 擴展

Business is booming, so he is planning to
expand his factory. (86 銘傳，84 交大，82 台大)

ex	+	pand
out	+	*spread*

ex	+	spire
out	+	*breathe*

expire 〔 ɪk'spaɪr 〕 v. 到期

When will the season ticket *expire*?

(91 台大)

•Check List•

(   ) 1. emphasize   A. jeopardize

(   ) 2. enchant   B. heighten

(   ) 3. endanger   C. exterminate

(   ) 4. endure   D. surpass

(   ) 5. enforce   E. inspect

(   ) 6. enhance   F. stress

(   ) 7. entertain   G. amuse

(   ) 8. eradicate   H. avoid

(   ) 9. erase   I. enlarge

(   ) 10. evade   J. terminate

(   ) 11. examine   K. implement

(   ) 12. exceed   L. remove

(   ) 13. exhibit   M. promote

(   ) 14. expand   N. display

(   ) 15. expire   O. tolerate

Vocabulary Ratings

5–7 *Good*   8–11 *Very Good*   12–15 *Excellent*

· Synonyms ·

1. emphasize
   = stress
   = highlight

2. enchant
   = fascinate

3. endanger
   = jeopardize
   = threaten

4. endure
   = tolerate
   = bear

5. enforce
   = implement

6. evade
   = avoid

7. eradicate
   = exterminate
   = destroy

8. entertain
   = amuse

9. erase
   = remove
   = wipe out

10. enhance
    = heighten

11. examine
    = inspect

12. exceed
    = surpass

13. exhibit
    = display

14. expand
    = enlarge
    = increase

15. expire
    = terminate

exploit 〔 ɪk'splɔɪt 〕 v. 剝削

During the period of colonization, many powerful countries *exploited* smaller countries. (83交大，81淡江)

expose 〔 ɪk'spoz 〕 v. 暴露

Don't *expose* yourself to the sun too long. It may do harm to your skin.

(82台大)

```
ex  + pose
 |      |
out + put
```

extend 〔 ɪk'stɛnd 〕 v. 伸出

We should *extend* a helping hand to a friend in need. (86逢甲，85中興，84成大，83交大)

F f

fade 〔 fed 〕 v. 褪色

This pair of jeans *faded* after being washed.

(85、82台大)

faint 〔 fent 〕 *v.* 暈倒

She screamed and *fainted* at the sight of the blood on the floor. (82 台大)

finance 〔 fəˈnæns 〕 *v.* 資助

Most magazines are *financed* with revenues from advertisements, subscription sales and newsstand sales. (85 交大)

flourish 〔ˈflɝɪʃ 〕 *v.* 興盛

If we get enough rain in the spring, the garden will *flourish*. (86 中興)

flour	+	ish
flower	+	*v.*

flush 〔 flʌʃ 〕 *v.* 臉紅

His face was *flushed* because he had run all the way from the dormitory. (85 清大)

frown 〔 fraʊn 〕 *v.* 皺眉

Why are you *frowning*? Is something bothering you? (87 中原，86 輔大，82 靜宜)

H h

heed〔 hid 〕 *v.* 注意

I told John not to drive without a helmet, but he did not *heed* my advice.（86文化）

hinder〔'hɪndɚ 〕 *v.* 妨礙

The disease *hinders* a plant's growth and leads to the death of the plant.（88中正，87淡江）

humiliate〔 hju'mɪlɪ,et 〕 *v.* 羞辱

Good sportsmanship requires that one not *humiliate* a defeated adversary.

（88政大，87中興，80淡江）

I i

identify〔 aɪ'dɛntə,faɪ 〕 *v.* 辨認

You can *identify* a culture by its body language.（81交大）

ignore 〔 ɪg'nor 〕 *v.* 忽視

If you *ignore* the traffic signals, you may have an accident. (88 中央，86 中原)

illuminate 〔 ɪ'lumə,net 〕 *v.* 照亮

Streetlights *illuminate* the road at night.

(87 逢甲)

il	+	lumin	+	ate
|		|		|
on	+	*light*	+	*v.*

illustrate 〔'ɪləstret 〕 *v.* 說明

The professor *illustrated* his point with an example. (86 中原、私醫)

imitate 〔'ɪmə,tet 〕 *v.* 模仿

Ann listened to her piano teacher play the music and then tried to *imitate* her. (86 中興)

immerse 〔 ɪ'mɝs 〕 v. 浸入

Our car was *immersed* in water during the flood. (86 輔大，82 台大)

```
im + merse
 |     |
in +  sink (沈)
```

impel 〔 ɪm'pɛl 〕 v. 驅使

Although the lawmaker did not want to run for office again, he was *impelled* to do so by the expectations of his supporters. (81 台大)

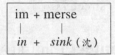

```
im + pel          im + pose
 |     |           |     |
in + drive        on +  put
```

impose 〔 ɪm'poz 〕 v. 強加

The government *imposes* a higher tax on the rich than on the poor. (87 成大)

imprison 〔 ɪm'prɪzn̩ 〕 v. 監禁

The man was *imprisoned* for burglary last year. (84 東吳)

indicate〔'ɪndə,ket〕 *v.* 指示

The arrow *indicates* that this is a one-way
street. (85 銘傳)

infect〔ɪn'fɛkt〕 *v.* 感染

Please cover your mouth when you cough so
that you do not *infect* others with your cold.

(89、86 輔大，85 台大)

inform〔ɪn'fɔrm〕 *v.* 通知

As his itinerary had been changed, he
informed the front desk that he would
leave early. (85 私醫，83 淡江)

inherit〔ɪn'hɛrɪt〕 *v.* 繼承

Ron's aunt didn't have any children, so
after she died, he *inherited* a large fortune.

(86 清大、銘傳，84 東吳，81 交大)

Check List

( ) 1. finance
( ) 2. flourish
( ) 3. flush
( ) 4. heed
( ) 5. hinder

( ) 6. humiliate
( ) 7. identify
( ) 8. ignore
( ) 9. illuminate
( ) 10. illustrate

( ) 11. imitate
( ) 12. immerse
( ) 13. impel
( ) 14. impose
( ) 15. inform

A. neglect
B. drive ; force
C. notice
D. recognize
E. sponsor

F. mimic ; copy
G. brighten
H. prosper
I. blush
J. notify

K. submerge
L. obstruct
M. explain
N. inflict
O. disgrace

Vocabulary Ratings

5–7 *Good*   8–11 *Very Good*   12–15 *Excellent*

Synonyms

1. immerse
   = submerge
   = dip

2. flourish
   = prosper
   = thrive

3. imitate
   = mimic = copy

4. heed
   = notice
   = pay attention to

5. hinder
   = obstruct
   = hold back

6. humiliate
   = disgrace

7. impel
   = drive = force

8. ignore
   = neglect
   = overlook

9. illuminate
   = brighten
   = light

10. illustrate
    = explain

11. flush
    = blush

12. finance
    = sponsor

13. identify
    = recognize

14. impose
    = inflict

15. inform
    = notify

initiate 〔 ɪˈnɪʃɪˌet 〕 v. 開始

Before *initiating* the new program, we made a careful plan. (87 政大，85 銘傳，80 淡江)

inquire 〔 ɪnˈkwaɪr 〕 v. 詢問

If you have any further questions, you may *inquire* at the information desk. (80 淡江)

in + quire	in + sert
| |	| |
in + *seek*	*in* + *put*

insert 〔 ɪnˈsɝt 〕 v. 挿入

He *inserted* the key into the lock and opened the door. (83 文化)

insist 〔 ɪnˈsɪst 〕 v. 堅持

Peter *insisted* that the new baby be named after his grandfather. (88、85 中正)

inspect 〔ɪnˈspɛkt〕 v. 檢查

The factory employs someone to *inspect* the
finished products for flaws.

（85 逢甲）

in	+	spect
into	+	look

inspire 〔ɪnˈspaɪr〕 v. 激起

The story of Helen Keller *inspired* many
people to work even harder.

（88 中央，87 中興，81 清大）

install 〔ɪnˈstɔl〕 v. 安裝

We plan to *install* an air conditioner in
our new home.

（85 台大）

in	+	stall
in	+	stand

instill 〔ɪnˈstɪl〕 v. 逐漸灌輸

Parents should gradually *instill* good
manners in their children. （85 台大，83 文化）

instruct 〔 ɪn'strʌkt 〕 v. 教導

My brother has promised to *instruct* me in
how to use the machine.

(89 成大，85 台大)

```
in + struct
 |      |
in + build
```

insult 〔 ɪn'sʌlt 〕 v. 侮辱

Ever since John *insulted* her, the teacher has
had it in for him. (84 政大，80 中興、淡江)

integrate 〔 'ɪntə͵gret 〕 v. 整合

If these immigrants want to be accepted by
our people, they should begin to *integrate*
into our society. (86 銘傳，85 逢甲)

intend 〔 ɪn'tɛnd 〕 v. 打算

I had *intended* to stay there for a week, but
due to an accident, I stayed there more than
a month. (86 中正)

intensify 〔 ɪn'tɛnsə،faɪ 〕 v. 加強

We must *intensify* our efforts in improving
the present situation.

（90 輔大，81 台大）

in	+	tens	+ ify
|		|	|
in	+	*stretch* +	*v.*

interfere 〔 ،ɪntɚ'fɪr 〕 v. 干涉

Human beings always *interfere* with nature.

（85 台大，84 台北大，82 輔大）

interrupt 〔 ،ɪntə'rʌpt 〕 v. 打斷

The operator *interrupted* and said that I had
already spoken three minutes. （85 台大，84 交大）

inter	+ rupt
|	|
between	+ *break*

in	+ vade
|	|
in	+ *go*

invade 〔 ɪn'ved 〕 v. 侵略

Ants *invaded* our kitchen so we called an
exterminator. （87 中正，86 中興）

invest 〔 ɪn'vɛst 〕 v. 投資

My uncle *invested* part of his savings in stocks. (88 政大、中央、銘傳，86 中興)

investigate 〔 ɪn'vɛstə,get 〕 v. 調查

If you hear such a rumor, *investigate* it thoroughly. (88 政大，87 中正，86 清大，83 文化)

involve 〔 ɪn'vɑlv 〕 v. 牽涉

Jack's new job *involves* a lot of business travel. (87 中央，86 成大)

```
in + volve
   |
in + roll
```

irritate 〔 'ɪrə,tet 〕 v. 激怒

He was *irritated* by the constant noise his neighbors made and called the police.

(88 中原，81 中興)

isolate 〔 'aɪsḷ,et 〕 v. 隔離

He had to be *isolated* because he came down with dengue fever. (86 銘傳，84 中興)

issue 〔ˈɪʃ ju 〕 v. 發行

The magazine is *issued* on the first day of every month. (87 中興，85 文化)

L l

launch 〔 lɔntʃ 〕 v. 發射

The spacecraft will be *launched* into space tomorrow. (86 清大)

legalize 〔ˈligl͵aɪz 〕 v. 使合法

Some people in the United States want to *legalize* abortion. (83 東吳)

lessen 〔ˈlɛsn̩ 〕 v. 減少

Hope *lessened* when six o'clock arrived and Jane had not appeared. (86 私醫，85 輔大)

loathe 〔 loð 〕 v. 厭惡

Cassius *loathed* Julius Caesar because Caesar was so rich and powerful. (84 交大)

•Check List•

(   ) 1. initiate   A. stimulate

(   ) 2. inquire   B. strengthen

(   ) 3. insist   C. concern

(   ) 4. inspire   D. reduce

(   ) 5. instruct   E. separate

(   ) 6. integrate   F. incorporate

(   ) 7. intensify   G. originate

(   ) 8. interfere   H. discontinue

(   ) 9. interrupt   I. release

(   ) 10. involve   J. ask ; question

(   ) 11. irritate   K. teach ; tutor

(   ) 12. isolate   L. hate ; dislike

(   ) 13. issue   M. annoy

(   ) 14. lessen   N. meddle

(   ) 15. loathe   O. persist

Vocabulary Ratings

5–7 *Good*   8–11 *Very Good*   12–15 *Excellent*

·Synonyms·

1. initiate
   = originate
   = start = begin

2. inquire = ask
   = question

3. loathe = hate
   = dislike

4. inspire
   = stimulate
   = arouse

5. instruct
   = teach = tutor

6. integrate
   = incorporate
   = combine

7. intensify
   = strengthen
   = build up

8. interfere
   = meddle

9. interrupt
   = discontinue

10. involve
    = concern

11. irritate
    = annoy
    = infuriate

12. isolate
    = separate

13. issue
    = release

14. lessen
    = reduce

15. insist
    = persist

M m

melt〔mɛlt〕v. 融化

In the spring when the snow *melts* there may be flooding. (85 台大、銘傳)

mend〔mɛnd〕v. 修補

It is never too late to *mend*. (84 成大)

monitor〔'mɑnətɚ〕v. 監視

In an honor system, there is no one to *monitor* the examination.

(88 政大，87 台大，85 中興，82 政大)

mumble〔'mʌmbḷ〕v. 喃喃地說

I cannot understand what you say when you *mumble*. Please speak up. (86 政大)

N n

notify ('notə,faɪ) v. 通知

If you continue to be absent from your classes, we will *notify* your parents.

(85 私醫，81 淡江)

not + ify
| |
mark + v.

O o

obstruct (əb'strʌkt) v. 阻礙

The large truck *obstructed* the road and no other vehicles could get by. (86 銘傳)

ob + struct
| |
against + build

order ('ɔrdə) v. 命令

The general *ordered* his men to march to the next town. (86 台大)

organize 〔'ɔrgən,aɪz〕 v. 組織

Just leave the arrangement of the meeting to him. He is very good at *organizing* things. (87 東吳)

originate 〔 ə'rɪdʒə,net 〕 v. 起源

Investigators found that the computer virus *originated* on a university campus. (86 逢甲)

overcome 〔,ovɚ'kʌm 〕 v. 克服

If you work hard, you will be able to *overcome* the difficulty in the end. (85 文化)

P p

penetrate 〔'pɛnə,tret〕 v. 穿透

The enemy have *penetrated* our second line of defense. (86 銘傳,83 文化)

perceive 〔 pɚˈsiv 〕 v. 察覺

Although it was still dark, I *perceived* that
morning was near when
I heard the rooster.

（84 交大）

per	+	ceive
through	+	take

perform 〔 pɚˈfɔrm 〕 v. 執行

He always *performs* his tasks well.

（85 中興，80 淡江）

permit 〔 pɚˈmɪt 〕 v. 允許

Slang is not generally *permitted* in published
scientific papers.

（82 私醫）

per	+	mit
through	+	send

persist 〔 pɚˈsɪst 〕 v. 堅持

If you *persist* until you complete the work,
you will feel very satisfied. （86 私醫）

persuade 〔 pɚˈswed 〕 v. 說服

Carol *persuaded* her parents that she was old enough to travel abroad alone.

（87台北大，86中興，84私醫，80成大）

ponder 〔ˈpɑndɚ〕 v. 思考

You should *ponder* the matter carefully before deciding. （84輔大）

postpone 〔 postˈpon 〕 v. 拖延

Never *postpone* until tomorrow what you can do today. （86逢甲，82、80中興）

post + pone	pre + dict
| |	| |
after + *put*	*before* + *say*

predict 〔 prɪˈdɪkt 〕 v. 預測

It is impossible to *predict* an earthquake.

（87中原，85文化、私醫）

prescribe 〔 prɪ'skraɪb 〕 v. 開藥方

The doctor *prescribed* some medicine
for her pain.

（85 私醫，81 淡江，80 中興）

```
pre    + scribe
 |        |
before + write
```

present 〔 prɪ'zɛnt 〕 v. 贈送

We *presented* Mother with some flowers
on Mother's Day. （86 中興）

preserve 〔 prɪ'zɝv 〕 v. 保存

This organization works hard to *preserve*
some historic buildings.

（88 台大，86 逢甲）

```
pre    + serve
 |        |
before + keep
```

prevail 〔 prɪ'vel 〕 v. 獲勝

Although we tried our best, the other team
prevailed and we lost the game. （85 台大、私醫）

·Check List·

(   ) 1. mend   A. feel ; sense

(   ) 2. monitor   B. forecast

(   ) 3. mumble   C. implement

(   ) 4. order   D. repair

(   ) 5. overcome   E. offer ; give

(   ) 6. penetrate   F. conquer

(   ) 7. perceive   G. consider

(   ) 8. perform   H. observe

(   ) 9. permit   I. allow ; let

(   ) 10. persuade   J. murmur

(   ) 11. ponder   K. convince

(   ) 12. postpone   L. command

(   ) 13. predict   M. triumph

(   ) 14. present   N. delay

(   ) 15. prevail   O. pierce

Vocabulary Ratings

5–7 *Good*   8–11 *Very Good*   12–15 *Excellent*

·Synonyms·

1. mend
   = repair = fix

2. monitor
   = observe
   = watch

3. mumble
   = murmur
   = mutter

4. order
   = command

5. overcome
   = conquer

6. predict
   = forecast
   = foresee

7. perform
   = implement
   = carry out

8. permit
   = allow = let

9. perceive
   = feel = sense

10. persuade
    = convince

11. ponder
    = consider
    = contemplate

12. postpone
    = delay
    = put off

13. penetrate
    = pierce

14. present
    = offer = give

15. prevail
    = triumph

probe 〔 prob 〕 *v.* 探索

An unmanned spacecraft was sent into space to *probe* the galaxy. (86私醫)

prohibit 〔 proˈhɪbɪt 〕 *v.* 禁止

They believe that nuclear weapons should be totally *prohibited*. (85中興，82文化)

prolong 〔 prəˈlɔŋ 〕 *v.* 延長

The meeting was *prolonged* by the lengthy speech of the chairman. (86逢甲)

promote 〔 prəˈmot 〕 *v.* 升職

Mr. Hu was *promoted* to the chief of the section due to his hard work.

(87中興、逢甲，86私醫)

pro	+	mote
forward	+	*move*

prosper 〔'prɑspɚ〕 *v.* 興盛

The business did not *prosper* and it soon closed. (86 中正)

publish 〔'pʌblɪʃ〕 *v.* 出版

His latest book will be *published* next month. (84 中興)

purify 〔'pjʊrəˌfaɪ〕 *v.* 使潔淨

You should *purify* the water because it may not be safe to drink.

(89 輔大，86 銘傳，80 淡江)

```
pur  + ify
 |      |
pure +  v.
```

pursue 〔 pɚ'su〕 *v.* 追求

She *pursued* the goal of perfection in her works. (86 交大)

R r

ravage 〔'rævɪdʒ〕 v. 破壞

Hurricanes *ravage* one spot; earthquakes destroy another. （86 中興）

recognize 〔'rɛkəg,naɪz〕 v. 認出

I did not *recognize* my old classmate because he looked completely different. （87 逢甲，86 中興）

recommend 〔,rɛkə'mɛnd〕 v. 推薦

My travel agent *recommended* this hotel.

（85 中正）

reconcile 〔'rɛkən,saɪl〕 v. 和解

The two friends had a terrible fight, but eventually they *reconciled*. （88 中正，86 成大）

recycle 〔ri'saɪkḷ〕 v. 回收

Some waste materials can be *recycled* and used again. （89 輔大，87 台北大，85 台大，80 淡江）

reflect〔rɪ'flɛkt〕v. 反射

Her image was *reflected* in the mirror.

（90 輔大，82 交大）

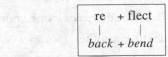

```
re   + flect
 |       |
back + bend
```

reform〔rɪ'fɔrm〕v. 改革

The government has promised to *reform* the education system so that students can learn more.（85 逢甲）

regulate〔'rɛgjə,let〕v. 調節

An air conditioner can *regulate* the temperature inside a room.（80 台大）

release〔rɪ'lis〕v. 釋放

After being in jail for ten years, the criminal was *released*.（87 台北大，87 文化）

relieve 〔 rɪ'liv 〕 v. 減輕

My headache was *relieved* after I took the painkiller. (91 台大，87 中興，86 私醫，85 中正)

remove 〔 rɪ'muv 〕 v. 清除

After the manager explained carefully to us how to carry out the project, all our doubts were *removed*. (86 中興，85 銘傳)

renew 〔 rɪ'nju 〕 v. 更新

I called a friend that I had not seen in many years and told him that I wanted to *renew* our friendship. (86 逢甲，81 台大)

renounce 〔 rɪ'naʊns 〕 v. 放棄

The governor *renounced* his office because of ill health. (82 淡江)

```
re   + nounce
 |       |
back + report
```

replace 〔 rɪˋples 〕 v. 取代

Nothing in the world can *replace* the love of parents for their children. (87 政大, 86 中興)

represent 〔 ͵rɛprɪˋzɛnt 〕 v. 代表

Wayne was chosen to *represent* our class at the ceremony. (87 政大)

require 〔 rɪˋkwaɪr 〕 v. 需要

To master a foreign language *requires* a lot of practice. (81 台大)

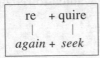

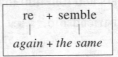

resemble 〔 rɪˋzɛmbļ 〕 v. 相像

Peter *resembles* his grandfather in many ways. (82 政大)

•Check List•

(   ) 1. probe   A. chase ; follow

(   ) 2. prohibit   B. forbid ; ban

(   ) 3. prolong   C. normalize

(   ) 4. promote   D. need ; want

(   ) 5. purify   E. settle

(   ) 6. pursue   F. explore

(   ) 7. ravage   G. substitute

(   ) 8. recommend   H. lengthen

(   ) 9. reconcile   I. improve

(   ) 10. recycle   J. cleanse

(   ) 11. reform   K. suggest

(   ) 12. regulate   L. reprocess

(   ) 13. renounce   M. advance

(   ) 14. replace   N. abandon

(   ) 15. require   O. wreck

Vocabulary Ratings

5–7 *Good*   8–11 *Very Good*   12–15 *Excellent*

·Synonyms·

1. probe
   = explore

2. prohibit
   = forbid = ban
   = outlaw

3. prolong
   = lengthen
   = elongate

4. promote
   = advance
   = upgrade

5. purify
   = cleanse

6. pursue
   = chase
   = follow

7. ravage
   = wreck
   = destroy

8. recommend
   = suggest

9. reconcile
   = settle

10. recycle
    = reprocess
    = reuse

11. reform
    = improve

12. regulate
    = normalize
    = control

13. renounce
    = abandon
    = desert

14. replace
    = substitute

15. require
    = need = want

resent 〔 rɪ'zɛnt 〕 *v.* 厭惡

He *resents* being imitated; so don't try to copy him. (87 交大)

reserve 〔 rɪ'zɝv 〕 *v.* 預訂

I'll call the restaurant and *reserve* a table for tonight. (86 政大，85 文化)

resign 〔 rɪ'zaɪn 〕 *v.* 辭職

Feeling that she was not cut out for the job, she decided to *resign*. (85 台大)

resist 〔 rɪ'zɪst 〕 *v.* 抵抗

I love chocolate; I can't *resist* the temptation of it. (86 交大、私醫)

re	+	sist
back	+	*stand*

resort 〔 rɪ'zɔrt 〕 *v.* 訴諸

We should *resort* to reason, not to violence, to solve problems. (89 淡江)

respond 〔 rɪ'spɑnd 〕 *v.* 回答

He *responded* to the question without
thinking. (87 中正，85 文化)

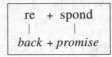

```
re  +  spond
 |       |
back + promise
```

restrain 〔 rɪ'stren 〕 *v.* 抑制

I *restrained* my desire to say what I thought.

(85 淡江，83 輔大，80 中興)

```
re  +   strain
 |        |
back + draw tight (拉緊)
```

restrict 〔 rɪ'strɪkt 〕 *v.* 限制

Our club membership is *restricted* to twelve.

(85 文化，84 政大)

resume 〔 rɪ'zum 〕 *v.* 恢復

No one can tell when Beijing will *resume*
the suspended cross-strait talks with Taipei.

(87 中正，87、86 中興)

retain〔rɪˋten〕*v.* 保留

He was able to *retain* his sense of humor in the embarrassing situation. (85中興)

retaliate〔rɪˋtælɪˏet〕*v.* 報復

The discontented publishers *retaliated* by boycotting the school bookstores. (83淡江)

retard〔rɪˋtɑrd〕*v.* 使遲緩

Chemicals are used to *retard* the growth of ornamental trees. (87台大,85銘傳)

retrieve〔rɪˋtriv〕*v.* 取回

To train his dog, Robert threw something far away and asked his dog to *retrieve* the object. (87台北大,81淡江)

re	+	trieve
again	+	*find*

reveal 〔 rɪ'vil 〕 v. 洩漏

Don't *reveal* to Helen that we are planning to go to the movie tonight.

(86 銘傳，85 文化，83 交大)

revenge 〔 rɪ'vɛndʒ 〕 v. 報復

He *revenges* himself on his persecutors.

(81 台大，80 淡江)

reverse 〔 rɪ'vɝs 〕 v. 使倒退

Looking over his shoulder, the taxi driver *reversed* the car down the street. (85 文化)

re	+ verse
back	+ turn

re	+ view
again	+ see

review 〔 rɪ'vju 〕 v. 複習

I make it a habit to *review* what I learn in class every day. (81 淡江)

revise 〔 rɪ'vaɪz 〕 v. 修改

Writers have to *revise* their manuscripts frequently. (83 文化，82 清大)

rotate 〔'rotet 〕 v. 旋轉

It takes the earth 24 hours to *rotate* 360 degrees. (86 中原)

rot	+ ate
turn	+ *v.*

ruin 〔'ruɪn 〕 v. 破壞

The incident *ruined* Mr. Smith's chances of becoming president. (81 清大)

S s

scatter 〔'skætɚ 〕 v. 散播

The wind *scattered* the papers around the room. (85 台大)

scold 〔 skold 〕 v. 責備

Tom was *scolded* by his boss for being late again. (85 台大)

scorn〔 skɔrn 〕 *v.* 輕視

You should not *scorn* those who need your help. (85文化)

shrink 〔 ʃrɪŋk 〕 *v.* 縮水

If wool is submerged in hot water, it tends to *shrink*. (84中興)

situate 〔 'sɪtʃu,et 〕 *v.* 位於

The U.S. Capitol building is *situated* in a small park surrounded by a number of government buildings. (82台大、私醫)

smuggle 〔 'smʌgl̩ 〕 *v.* 走私

They tried to *smuggle* refugees into the country. (84文化)

snore 〔 snor 〕 *v.* 打鼾

Mr. Wang *snores* so loudly that Mrs. Wang can't sleep. (85淡江)

Check List

( ) 1. resign   A. maintain ; keep

( ) 2. resist   B. blame

( ) 3. retaliate   C. quit ; step down

( ) 4. respond   D. inhibit

( ) 5. restrain   E. amend

( ) 6. restrict   F. fight

( ) 7. resume   G. disclose

( ) 8. retain   H. spread

( ) 9. reveal   I. restart

( )10. revise   J. revenge

( )11. rotate   K. reply ; answer

( )12. scatter   L. revolve

( )13. scold   M. locate

( )14. scorn   N. confine ; limit

( )15. situate   O. belittle

Vocabulary Ratings

5–7 *Good*   8–11 *Very Good*   12–15 *Excellent*

·Synonyms·

1. resign
   = quit
   = step down

2. resist
   = fight

3. retaliate
   = revenge

4. respond
   = reply
   = answer

5. restrain
   = inhibit
   = hold back

6. restrict
   = confine
   = limit

7. resume
   = restart
   = start again

8. retain
   = maintain
   = keep

9. revise
   = amend

10. rotate
    = revolve

11. scatter
    = spread

12. scold
    = blame
    = tell off

13. scorn
    = belittle
    = despise

14. situate
    = locate

15. reveal
    = disclose

soothe 〔 suð 〕 *v.* 緩和

I put some ice on the burn to *soothe* the pain. (86 逢甲)

specify 〔 ˈspɛsəˌfaɪ 〕 *v.* 詳述

Electrical energy may be divided into two components *specified* as positive and negative. (85 銘傳)

speculate 〔 ˈspɛkjəˌlet 〕 *v.* 猜測

I don't know how many students will pass the exam. I can only *speculate*. (85 逢甲)

spoil 〔 spɔɪl 〕 *v.* 破壞

The party was *spoiled* by the fight between Jack and Peter. (85 政大)

sprain 〔 spren 〕 *v.* 扭傷

I slipped on the icy road and *sprained* my ankle. (81 淡江)

startle 〔'stɑrtḷ〕 v. 使驚訝

I was *startled* when Billy suddenly appeared at the door. (81 交大，80 輔大)

stick 〔 stɪk 〕 v. 堅持

Promising young men always *stick* to their ideals and never give up. (86 銘傳)

stiffen 〔'stɪfən〕 v. 硬化

This product will *stiffen* your hair and keep it from moving. (86 中興)

stimulate 〔'stɪmjə‚let 〕 v. 刺激

The good smell from the kitchen *stimulated* my appetite. (87 中興，85 台大、清大)

stun 〔 stʌn 〕 v. 使目瞪口呆

They were *stunned* by her beauty and stood there speechless. (87 淡江)

subject 〔 səb'dʒɛkt 〕 v. 使遭受

People who take on a second job inevitably *subject* themselves to greater stress. (84 台大)

submit 〔 səb'mɪt 〕 v. 提出

Kelly & Smith was the only firm to *submit* a bid. (83 文化．81 台大)

subside 〔 səb'saɪd 〕 v. 消退

The flood caused by the typhoon *subsided* three days later. (81 台大)

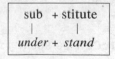

substitute 〔 'sʌbstə,tjut 〕 v. 代替

Since we have run out of honey, we *substitute* sugar for it. (81 淡江)

supplement 〔'sʌplə‚mɛnt 〕 v. 補充

The doctor asked me to take a multivitamin to *supplement* my diet. (85 逢甲)

surpass 〔 sə'pæs 〕 v. 超越

May got 95 on the history exam, but Tom *surpassed* her with a 97. (80 台大)

surround 〔 sə'raʊnd 〕 v. 包圍

When the young singer appeared, he was *surrounded* by hundreds of his fans.

(87 政大)

suspect 〔 sə'spɛkt 〕 v. 懷疑

I am not sure who stole the radio, but I *suspect* our neighbor's children.

(85 中興)

su	+	spect
under	+	*see*

suspend 〔 sə'spɛnd 〕 *v.* 暫停

The students caught cheating on the test were *suspended* from school for one week.

（86 輔大）

sympathize 〔'sɪmpə,θaɪz 〕 *v.* 同情

Although I *sympathized* with John's misfortune, there was little I could do to help him. （86 銘傳）

T t

tease 〔 tiz 〕 *v.* 嘲笑

Stop *teasing* him. He is merely a kid. （85 文化）

terminate 〔'tɝmə,net 〕 *v.* 終止

We decided to *terminate* the contract with him due to his misbehavior.

（86 輔大、中原、逢甲，85 台大）

term + inate
| |
limit + *v.*

testify 〔'tɛstə,faɪ 〕 *v.* 作證

The witness *testified* in court, describing what he saw when the bank was robbed.

（86 中正）

threaten 〔'θrɛtn̩ 〕 *v.* 威脅

The woman was *threatened* by the robber, so she gave him her purse.

（85 台大，84 輔大，82 東吳）

thrive 〔 θraɪv 〕 *v.* 興盛

The industry is *thriving* in this area due to the support of the government. （86 中興）

tolerate 〔'tɑlə,ret 〕 *v.* 忍受

He moved out because he could not *tolerate* his roommate's friends.

（90 輔大，87 中原，82、80 中興，81 清大，80 淡江）

·Check List·

(   ) 1. soothe   A. encircle

(   ) 2. speculate   B. pity ; feel for

(   ) 3. spoil   C. dumbfound

(   ) 4. sprain   D. wrench ; twist

(   ) 5. stick   E. attest

(   ) 6. stiffen   F. menace

(   ) 7. stun   G. pacify ; ease

(   ) 8. submit   H. adjourn

(   ) 9. supplement   I. guess

(   ) 10. surround   J. solidify

(   ) 11. suspend   K. complement

(   ) 12. sympathize   L. ruin

(   ) 13. tease   M. cling ; adhere

(   ) 14. testify   N. present

(   ) 15. threaten   O. mock

Vocabulary Ratings

5–7 *Good*   8–11 *Very Good*   12–15 *Excellent*

·Synonyms·

1. soothe
   = pacify
   = calm = ease

2. speculate
   = guess

3. spoil
   = ruin

4. sprain
   = wrench
   = twist

5. stick
   = cling
   = adhere

6. stiffen
   = solidify
   = harden

7. stun
   = dumbfound
   = daze

8. submit
   = present
   = offer

9. supplement
   = complement

10. surround
    = encircle
    = enclose

11. suspend
    = adjourn
    = halt

12. sympathize
    = pity = feel for

13. tease = mock
    = make fun of

14. testify
    = attest

15. threaten
    = menace

transfer 〔 træns'fɜ 〕 *v.* 轉移

He was *transferred* from Taipei to Hong
Kong. (85 文化、逢甲)

trans	+	fer
across	+	*carry*

transmit 〔 træns'mɪt 〕 *v.* 傳送

The radio station *transmits* its program over
the airwaves. (87 中原，86 中正，85 逢甲，82 交大，81 台大)

transport 〔 træns'port 〕 *v.* 運送

The goods were *transported* by ship to
Keelung Harbor.

(85 逢甲，82 交大)

trans	+	port
across	+	*carry*

trigger 〔 'trɪgɚ 〕 *v.* 引發

It is possible that an emotional condition
can *trigger* a physical reaction. (86 銘傳)

U u

undergo 〔͵ʌndɚˈgo 〕 v. 經歷

All newcomers in this company have to
undergo some job training. (86 文化)

unearth 〔 ʌnˈ3θ 〕 v. 挖掘

The remains of dinosaurs were first
unearthed by North American settlers. (84 交大)

utilize 〔ˈjutl͵aɪz 〕 v. 利用

You should *utilize* your abilities to the full.

(85 淡江)

V v

vanish 〔ˈvænɪʃ 〕 v. 消失

Peter suddenly *vanished*; no one knew where
he had gone.

(85 私醫，84 成大，82 政大，80 淡江)

van	+	ish
|		|
empty	+	*v.*

vibrate ['vaɪbret] *v.* 震動

The roar of a jet plane *vibrated* the
windowpanes.

（85 輔大、淡江）

```
vibra + (a)te
  |         |
shake  +    v.
```

W w

whisper ['hwɪspɚ] *v.* 低語

The child *whispered* to his mother so that
his father would not hear. （86 政大，82 靜宜）

withdraw [wɪð'drɔ] *v.* 退縮

On touching the hot pot, he *withdrew* his
hand immediately. （86 中興，82 東吳）

```
with + draw
  |      |
against + 拉
```

形容詞

absurd 〔 əb'sɝd 〕 *adj.* 荒謬的

The performer's *absurd* behavior made the audience laugh. (82交大，81清大，80逢甲)

abundant 〔 ə'bʌndənt 〕 *adj.* 豐富的

Oil is *abundant* in this area. (84交大)

academic 〔 ,ækə'dɛmɪk 〕 *adj.* 學術的

His *academic* performance is poor; he usually gets bad grades. (88政大)

accurate 〔 'ækjərɪt 〕 *adj.* 精確的

His *accurate* prediction saved many people's lives and property.

(85台大)

ac	+	cur	+ ate
to	+	take care	+ adj.

accustomed 〔 ə'kʌstəmd 〕 *adj.* 習慣的

After a week, she got *accustomed* to life in the new school. (85文化)

acute 〔 ə'kjut 〕 *adj.* 急性的

The patient was suffering from *acute* stomach ulcer. (86輔大)

addicted 〔 ə'dɪktɪd 〕 *adj.* 上癮的

Those *addicted* to drugs may do whatever it takes to get drugs. (87逢甲，86私醫，83淡江)

adverse 〔 əd'vɜs 〕 *adj.* 不利的

Adverse conditions forced the climbing party to turn back. (86中正)

ad + verse
| |
to + turn

aggressive 〔 əˈgrɛsɪv 〕 *adj.* 有攻擊性的

Killer bees are more *aggressive* than other types of bees and are very dangerous.

（88 中正，87 逢甲，86 中興，82 文化）

```
ag  +  gress  +  ive
|       |        |
to  +  walk  +  adj.
```

agreeable 〔 əˈgriəbḷ 〕 *adj.* 和氣的

His employer appeared to be in such an *agreeable* mood that Tom decided to ask for a raise. （81 淡江）

allergic 〔 əˈlɝdʒɪk 〕 *adj.* 過敏的

He is *allergic* to dust and so he often sneezes. （88 中央）

amateur 〔 ˈæməˌtʃʊr 〕 *adj.* 業餘的

Mr. Shaw is an *amateur* photographer.

（81 台大，80 輔大）

Check List

( )	1. transmit	A. experience
( )	2. transport	B. ridiculous
( )	3. trigger	C. precise ; exact
( )	4. undergo	D. tremble ; shake
( )	5. unearth	E. convey ; send
( )	6. utilize	F. opposing
( )	7. vanish	G. dig
( )	8. vibrate	H. carry ; ship
( )	9. absurd	I. educational
( )	10. abundant	J. activate
( )	11. academic	K. make use of
( )	12. accurate	L. friendly
( )	13. addicted	M. plentiful
( )	14. adverse	N. hooked
( )	15. agreeable	O. disappear

Vocabulary Ratings

5-7 *Good*   8-11 *Very Good*   12-15 *Excellent*

·Synonyms·

1. transmit
   = convey
   = send

2. transport
   = carry = ship

3. trigger
   = activate
   = cause

4. undergo
   = experience
   = go through

5. unearth
   = dig
   = excavate

6. utilize
   = make use of

7. accurate
   = precise
   = exact
   = correct

8. abundant
   = plentiful
   = rich

9. vanish
   = disappear

10. vibrate
    = tremble
    = shake

11. absurd
    = ridiculous

12. academic
    = educational

13. addicted
    = hooked

14. adverse
    = opposing
    = unfavorable

15. agreeable
    = friendly

ambiguous (æm′bɪgjuəs) *adj.* 模稜兩可的

His remarks were *ambiguous*. We were not sure what he meant. (85 逢甲、私醫，84 交大，82 文化)

anonymous (ə′nɑnəməs) *adj.* 匿名的

Most traditional folk songs are of *anonymous* origin. (91 台大，85 銘傳)

an	+ onym	+ ous
|	|	|
without	*+ name*	*+ adj.*

ant(e)	+ ique
|	|
before	*+ adj.*

antique (æn′tik) *adj.* 古董的

The apartment was decorated with *antique* furniture. (86、82 清大)

anxious (′æŋkʃəs) *adj.* 憂慮的

He feels *anxious* about his future.

(85 清大，81 交大)

appealing 〔 ə'piliŋ 〕 *adj.* 吸引人的

Your suggestion is very *appealing*, but there are difficulties involved. (81 清大)

appropriate 〔 ə'propriɪt 〕 *adj.* 適當的

Screaming doesn't seem to be an *appropriate* response to this situation. (82 中興)

arrogant 〔 'ærəgənt 〕 *adj.* 自大的

Mr. Dale is very *arrogant*, always considering himself better than others.

(85 中興)

artificial 〔 ˌɑrtə'fɪʃəl 〕 *adj.* 人造的

There was an *artificial* Chrismas tree standing near the door.

(85 銘傳,90、80 輔大)

art +	ific +	ial
art +	do +	adj.

authentic 〔ɔ'θɛntɪk 〕*adj.* 眞正的

Consumers should be sure that the drugs they buy contain *authentic* ingredients.

（89輔大，85私醫，84中興）

awkward 〔'ɔkwəd 〕*adj.* 笨拙的

Tom is terribly shy and he feels *awkward* in the presence of women.

（86輔大，82中興）

awk	+	ward
wrong	+	*adj.*

B b

barbarous 〔'barbərəs 〕*adj.* 野蠻的

The natives on that small island were still primitive and *barbarous*. （82文化）

barren 〔'bærən 〕*adj.* 不毛的

The desert area is dry and *barren* and can't grow any crop. （89輔大，86銘傳）

beneficial 〔͵bɛnə'fɪʃəl〕 *adj.* 有益的

There are thousands of kinds of bacteria, many of which are *beneficial*.

（88 台大，86 清大，84 私醫，83 中興）

```
bene + fic + ial
 |      |     |
good +  do  + adj.
```

blunt 〔blʌnt〕 *adj.* 鈍的

The knife is *blunt*. It doesn't cut well. （82 文化）

bold 〔bold〕 *adj.* 大膽的

The writer is famous for her *bold* style of writing. （86 中興）

brave 〔brev〕 *adj.* 勇敢的

He works in the most dangerous prison in the country. He is a *brave* man.

（89 成大，85 淡江）

brilliant 〔'brɪljənt 〕 *adj.* 傑出的

She is truly a *brilliant* musician; you should come to listen to her for yourself. （86 銘傳）

C c

capable 〔'kcpəbḷ 〕 *adj.* 能夠的

Susan isn't really *capable* of riding a bicycle yet. （83 文化）

casual 〔'kæʒuəl 〕 *adj.* 輕便的

It is really just a *casual* gathering; don't dress up. （87 政大，86 私醫）

chronic 〔'krɑnɪk 〕 *adj.* 慢性的

Diabetes is a *chronic* disease and will greatly influence a person's health.

（86 私醫）

chron	+	ic
|		|
time	+	*adj.*

clumsy 〔ˈklʌmzɪ〕 adj. 笨拙的

Peter was *clumsy* at using a knife and fork while having a steak. (83 文化)

coherent 〔koˈhɪrənt〕 adj. 連貫的

We found the professor's talk on nuclear reactors quite *coherent*. (81 中興)

co	+ her	+ ent
|	|	|
together	+ *stick* (黏)	+ *adj.*

competent 〔ˈkɑmpətənt〕 adj. 能幹的

You need a very *competent* production manager to lead the section. (85、84 文化)

complex 〔kəmˈplɛks〕 adj. 複雜的

The problem is too *complex* to be solved in a short time. (86 逢甲，82 文化，80 東吳)

·Check List·

(   ) 1. ambiguous   A. uncivilized

(   ) 2. anonymous   B. courageous

(   ) 3. anxious   C. conceited

(   ) 4. appealing   D. consistent

(   ) 5. appropriate   E. genuine ; true

(   ) 6. arrogant   F. equivocal

(   ) 7. authentic   G. unidentified

(   ) 8. awkward   H. sterile

(   ) 9. barbarous   I. tempting

(   ) 10. barren   J. dull

(   ) 11. beneficial   K. clumsy

(   ) 12. blunt   L. suitable

(   ) 13. brave   M. skillful

(   ) 14. brilliant   N. concerned

(   ) 15. coherent   O. advantageous

Vocabulary Ratings

5–7 *Good*   8–11 *Very Good*   12–15 *Excellent*

·Synonyms·

1. ambiguous
   = equivocal
   = vague

2. barren
   = sterile
   = infertile

3. anxious
   = concerned
   = nervous

4. appealing
   = tempting
   = attractive

5. appropriate
   = suitable
   = fitting

6. arrogant
   = conceited
   = haughty

7. blunt
   = dull

8. authentic
   = genuine
   = true

9. awkward
   = clumsy

10. barbarous
    = uncivilized

11. anonymous
    = unidentified
    = nameless

12. beneficial
    = advantageous

13. brave
    = courageous
    = fearless

14. brilliant
    = skillful

15. coherent
    = consistent

complicated (ˈkɑmpləˌketɪd) *adj.* 複雜的

A *complicated* maze of tunnels runs beneath the main pyramid. (86中正,85文化)

compulsory (kəmˈpʌlsərɪ) *adj.* 必要的

In a formal paper it is *compulsory* to use footnotes each time a source is quoted.

(86逢甲,84輔大)

com	+ puls	+ ory
with	drive	adj.

conceivable (kənˈsivəbḷ) *adj.* 可想像的

We have tried every *conceivable* solution. However, the problem remains unsolved.

(80淡江)

concise (kənˈsaɪs) *adj.* 簡潔的

You had better be *concise* when writing an English composition.

(84交大)

con	+ cise
all	cut

confidential 〔ˌkɑnfəˈdɛnʃəl〕 *adj.* 機密的

The information is *confidential*. Never ever tell anyone about it. (85 文化，82 輔大)

conservative 〔kənˈsɝvətɪv〕 *adj.* 保守的

Punk rock fashions never caught on in this town; residents are too *conservative*.

(88 政大，87 逢甲，85 文化)

considerable 〔kənˈsɪdərəbḷ〕 *adj.* 相當大的

Our company's profits increased last year by a *considerable* amount.

(86 銘傳，84 政大，81 清大)

considerate 〔kənˈsɪdərɪt〕 *adj.* 體貼的

It was not *considerate* of you to treat him so coldly. (86 輔大)

constitutional 〔͵kɑnstə'tjuʃənḷ 〕 *adj.*

憲法的

There are strict *constitutional* limits on the president's power. (86 銘傳)

con + stitut + ion + al
all + stand + n. + adj.

constructive 〔 kən'strʌktɪv 〕 *adj.*

建設性的

He always gives *constructive* advice. (82 東吳)

contagious 〔 kən'tedʒəs 〕 *adj.* 傳染的

Many people believe eating garlic protects one from viruses and bacteria that spread *contagious* diseases. (89 輔大，86 中正)

con + tagi + ous
together + touch + adj.

contaminated 〔kənˈtæməˌnetɪd〕 adj.
受到污染的

Many people were hospitalized after drinking *contaminated* water. (89 輔大，80 淡江)

contemporary 〔kənˈtɛmpəˌrɛrɪ〕 adj.
現代的

Young people usually prefer *contemporary* music to that of their parents' generation.

(86 成大)

contradictory 〔ˌkɑntrəˈdɪktərɪ〕 adj.
矛盾的

Their answers were mutually *contradictory*. We didn't know whose was right. (84 文化)

contra	+ dict	+ ory
against	+ *say*	+ *adj.*

controversial〔͵kɑntrə'vɝʃəl〕 *adj.*

有爭議的

Abortion is a *controversial* issue. Some are for it; some are against it.

（88 政大，86 中原、逢甲，81 政大）

contro	+ vers	+ ial
against	+ *turn*	+ *adj.*

conventional〔kən'vɛnʃənḷ〕*adj.* 傳統的

James is too *conventional* a guy to be interested in a crazy idea like that.

（89 成大，85 政大）

counterfeit〔'kɑʊntɚfɪt〕*adj.* 偽造的

A large amount of *counterfeit* money was discovered at the scene.

（84 政大）

counter	+ feit
against	+ *make*

courteous 〔ˈkɝtɪəs 〕 *adj.* 有禮貌的

You should be *courteous* when talking to
your superiors. (87中興、中原、文化)

cozy 〔ˈkozɪ 〕 *adj.* 舒適的

We felt comfortable sitting together by the
fire in our *cozy* little living room. (86銘傳)

creative 〔 krɪˈetɪv 〕 *adj.* 有創意的

During the summers at the lake, the artist
did some of her most *creative* work. (86輔大)

critical 〔ˈkrɪtɪkḷ 〕 *adj.* 決定性的

Your help was *critical* to his success; without
you, he would have failed. (85交大，86、85中興)

cunning 〔ˈkʌnɪŋ 〕 *adj.* 狡猾的

She is as *cunning* as a fox; if I were you,
I'd be careful. (86中興，81淡江)

Check List

(   ) 1. complicated   A. infectious

(   ) 2. compulsory   B. debatable

(   ) 3. conceivable   C. polite

(   ) 4. concise   D. complex

(   ) 5. conservative   E. sly ; crafty

(   ) 6. considerable   F. thoughtful

(   ) 7. contagious   G. essential

(   ) 8. contaminated   H. original

(   ) 9. controversial   I. polluted

(   ) 10. counterfeit   J. imaginable

(   ) 11. courteous   K. decisive

(   ) 12. cozy   L. brief ; clear

(   ) 13. creative   M. fake ; forged

(   ) 14. critical   N. comfortable

(   ) 15. cunning   O. conventional

| Vocabulary Ratings |

5–7 *Good*   8–11 *Very Good*   12–15 *Excellent*

·Synonyms·

1. controversial
   = debatable

2. courteous
   = polite

3. cozy
   = comfortable

4. conceivable
   = imaginable

5. conservative
   = conventional
   = traditional

6. considerate
   = thoughtful
   = understanding

7. contagious
   = infectious
   = communicable

8. contaminated
   = polluted

9. complicated
   = complex

10. counterfeit
    = fake
    = forged

11. compulsory
    = essential
    = necessary
    = obliged

12. concise
    = brief = clear

13. creative
    = original
    = innovative

14. critical
    = decisive
    = crucial

15. cunning
    = sly = crafty

curious (ˈkjʊrɪəs) *adj.* 好奇的

He is interested in everything; he is a *curious*
reader. (86 銘傳，83 淡江)

cur	+	ious
take care	+	*adj.*

D d

damp (dæmp) *adj.* 潮濕的

Everything is *damp* in rainy weather. (85 交大)

dazzling (ˈdæzlɪŋ) *adj.* 燦爛的

Jewelry, such as gold and diamond, is as
dazzling as it is expensive. (86 銘傳)

decent (ˈdisn̩t) *adj.* 合宜的

Miss Grace is always dressed in a *decent*
manner. (85 清大，84 交大)

dejected 〔 dɪˈdʒɛktɪd 〕 *adj.* 沮喪的

After losing the competition, Ed was
dejected for days.

（85 清大，84 淡江）

de	+ ject	+ ed
|	|	|
down	+ *throw*	+ *adj.*

delicate 〔ˈdɛləkət〕 *adj.* 精緻的

The shirt made of *delicate* silk is costly. （84 交大）

delirious 〔 dɪˈlɪrɪəs 〕 *adj.* 精神錯亂的

The patient was *delirious*; what he said
made no sense. （85 銘傳）

dependent 〔 dɪˈpɛndənt 〕 *adj.* 依賴的

He is still *dependent* on his parents since he
is under 18. （87、86 逢甲）

determined 〔 dɪˈtɝmɪnd 〕 *adj.* 堅決的

Whether you agree or not, he is *determined*
to do it. （87 東吳）

diligent ('dɪlədʒənt) *adj.* 勤勉的

He is a *diligent* student who spares no effort in his studies. (86 中興，85 清大)

dim (dɪm) *adj.* 昏暗的

The light was too *dim* for the boy to read the book. (82 靜宜)

disabled (dɪs'ebḷd) *adj.* 殘障的

The bus has been designed to accommodate *disabled* passengers. (85 銘傳)

disposable (dɪ'spozəbḷ) *adj.* 用完即可丟的

Our rivers have been polluted by many *disposable* objects, such as paper cups, boxes, etc.

(85 台大，86 銘傳)

dis	+ pos	+ able
away	+ *put*	+ *adj.*

distinct 〔dɪ'stɪŋkt〕 *adj.* 清楚的

There is a *distinct* difference between the two objects. (87中原，85淡江，84輔大)

distinctive 〔dɪ'stɪŋktɪv〕 *adj.* 獨特的

A *distinctive* feature of the car is its all leather interior. (85淡江)

distracting 〔dɪ'stræktɪŋ〕 *adj.* 令人分心的

Mike finds it *distracting* to study and listen to music at the same time. (85東吳)

diversified 〔də'vɝsə,faɪd〕 *adj.* 多樣的

It is difficult to describe a "typical American family" because the U.S. is such a *diversified* country. (86交大、銘傳，82淡江)

dizzy 〔'dɪzɪ〕 *adj.* 暈眩的

The children ran in a circle until they felt *dizzy*. (84文化)

dogmatic〔dɔg'mætɪk〕 *adj.* 武斷的

My father is *dogmatic* in his opinions; he'll never change his mind. (86 中正，84 交大)

dominant 〔'dɑmənənt〕 *adj.* 支配的

The Kuomintang used to be the *dominant* party in Taiwan. (87 交大)

domin + ant	dorm + ant
| |	| |
rule + *adj.*	*sleep* + *adj.*

dormant 〔'dɔrmənt〕 *adj.* 休止的

The volcano has lain *dormant* for several centuries. (86 中正)

drastic 〔'dræstɪk〕 *adj.* 激烈的

The measure the government took seemed too *drastic* for some people to accept.

(87 政大，83 中興)

drowsy [ˈdraʊzɪ] *adj.* 想睡的

Because I stayed up late last night, I felt *drowsy* this morning. (84 成大，80 淡江、文化)

duplicate [ˈdjupləkɪt] *adj.* 複製的

Modern printing equipment quickly turns out *duplicate* copies of textual and pictorial matter. (86 中原)

du	+ plic	+ ate
two	+ fold	+ adj.

E e

eccentric [ɪkˈsɛntrɪk] *adj.* 古怪的

Ann is such an *eccentric* girl that no one likes to be with her.

(89 輔大，81 清大)

ec	+ centr	+ ic
out	+ center	+ adj.

economic [ˌikəˈnɑmɪk] *adj.* 經濟的

We consider the government's *economic* policy correct. (87 政大，82 逢甲)

·Check List·

(   ) 1. curious   A. industrious

(   ) 2. damp   B. depressed

(   ) 3. dazzling   C. inquisitive

(   ) 4. decent   D. resolute ; firm

(   ) 5. dejected   E. moist ; humid

(   ) 6. delicate   F. characteristic

(   ) 7. dependent   G. odd ; weird

(   ) 8. determined   H. bright

(   ) 9. diligent   I. sleepy ; dozy

(   ) 10. dim   J. noticeable

(   ) 11. distinct   K. proper

(   ) 12. distinctive   L. radical

(   ) 13. drastic   M. refined

(   ) 14. drowsy   N. shadowy

(   ) 15. eccentric   O. reliant

Vocabulary Ratings

5–7 *Good*   8–11 *Very Good*   12–15 *Excellent*

·Synonyms·

1. curious
   = inquisitive

2. damp
   = moist = wet
   = humid

3. dazzling
   = bright
   = glaring

4. decent
   = proper
   = adequate

5. dejected
   = depressed
   = gloomy

6. delicate
   = refined

7. determined
   = resolute
   = firm

8. dependent
   = reliant

9. diligent
   = industrious

10. dim = dark
    = shadowy

11. distinct
    = noticeable
    = clear

12. distinctive
    = characteristic
    = typical

13. drastic
    = radical
    = extreme

14. drowsy
    = sleepy = dozy

15. eccentric
    = odd = weird

economical 〔͵ikə'nɑmɪkl̩〕 *adj.* 節省的

Since I don't have much money, I try to be *economical*. (88 台大，86 政大，83 輔大，80 東吳)

effective 〔ə'fɛktɪv〕 *adj.* 有效的

Try to make *effective* use of your time during an exam. (86 銘傳)

energetic 〔͵ɛnə'dʒɛtɪk〕 *adj.* 精力充沛的

Mr. Kwan established a reputation as a hard-working, no-nonsense, and *energetic* leader.

(83 淡江)

engrossed 〔ɪn'grost〕 *adj.* 專心的

Mrs. Wilson was completely *engrossed* in her work and didn't hear me come in.

(85 銘傳)

enormous 〔 ɪ'nɔrməs 〕 *adj.* 巨大的

The construction was estimated to cost an *enormous* amount of money. (86 銘傳，85 輔大)

```
e  + norm + ous
|      |      |
out + 標準  + adj.
```

equivalent 〔 ɪ'kwɪvələnt 〕 *adj.* 相等的

One U.S. dollar is *equivalent* to 34 New Taiwan dollars. (86、81 政大)

```
equi + val + ent
 |      |     |
equal + worth + adj.
```

essential 〔 ə'sɛnʃəl 〕 *adj.* 必要的

I need your help. Your support is *essential* to my success. (87、86 中興，86 逢甲)

ethnic 〔'ɛθnɪk 〕 *adj.* 民族的

Canada and the U.S. are composed of diverse *ethnic* groups. (86 逢甲、私醫)

exceptional ﹝ ɪk'sɛpʃənḷ ﹞ *adj.* 非凡的

The actors' performances were praised as
exceptional.（86 銘傳）

ex	+ cept	+ ion	+ al
out	+ take	+ n.	+ adj.

excessive ﹝ ɪk'sɛsɪv ﹞ *adj.* 過度的

He accused the police of using *excessive*
force to stop the demonstration.

（86 中原、銘傳，81 淡江）

ex	+ cess	+ ive
out	+ go	+ adj.

exhausted ﹝ ɪg'zɔstɪd ﹞ *adj.* 筋疲力盡的

Please let me sit down. I'm *exhausted*!

（87 淡江）

exotic ﹝ ɪg'zɑtɪk ﹞ *adj.* 有異國情調的

The ornaments I bought in the local
Hawaiian shop look *exotic* and beautiful.

（88 銘傳）

extensive 〔 ɪk'stɛnsɪv 〕 *adj.* 廣泛的

The institute is conducting *extensive* research on the side effects of the drug.

（87中正，86清大）

ex	+ tens	+ ive
|	|	|
out	+ *stretch*	+ *adj.*

external 〔 ɪk'stɜnl̩ 〕 *adj.* 外部的

This cream is for *external* use only. （83淡江）

extinct 〔 ɪk'stɪŋkt 〕 *adj.* 絕種的

Many kinds of rare plants and animals have become *extinct*. （87中原，83交大，82輔大，80逢甲）

extravagant 〔 ɪk'strævəgənt 〕 *adj.* 奢侈的

To have a meal at the Sherwood Hotel is *extravagant*. （88銘傳）

extra	+ vaga	+ (a)nt
|	|	|
beyond	+ *wander*	+ *adj.*

F f

faithful 〔'feθfəl 〕 *adj.* 忠實的

He was always *faithful* to her despite her behavior. (85 台大)

fantastic 〔 fæn'tæstɪk 〕 *adj.* 極好的

The performance of the musician was *fantastic*. We enjoyed it very much. (82 文化)

fatal 〔'fetḷ 〕 *adj.* 致命的

The wound is *fatal*. I doubt if he can survive until morning. (87 東吳)

fearful 〔'fɪrfəl 〕 *adj.* 害怕的

We are *fearful* that the river will flood if it keeps raining. (85 台大)

feasible 〔'fizəbḷ〕 adj. 可行的

With the advance in technical knowledge, a manned flight to Mars may be *feasible* in the future. (88 中原,83 交大)

```
feas + ible
 |      |
 do  + adj.
```

feeble 〔'fibḷ〕 adj. 虛弱的

The old lady is *feeble*; she can't walk without a stick. (84 成大)

fertile 〔'fɜtḷ〕 adj. 肥沃的

The farmland is *fertile* and it is expected to produce a good harvest. (89 輔大,86 淡江)

flexible 〔'flɛksəbḷ〕 adj. 有彈性的

Rubber is a kind of *flexible* material.

(87 中興,82 文化)

```
flex + ible
 |      |
bend + adj.
```

·Check List·

(   ) 1. economical   A. loyal ; devoted

(   ) 2. energetic   B. practicable

(   ) 3. engrossed   C. extraordinary

(   ) 4. enormous   D. frugal ; thrifty

(   ) 5. equivalent   E. equal

(   ) 6. ethnic   F. scared ; afraid

(   ) 7. exceptional   G. vigorous

(   ) 8. exhausted   H. terrific

(   ) 9. extensive   I. wide-ranging

(   ) 10. faithful   J. racial

(   ) 11. fantastic   K. absorbed

(   ) 12. fatal   L. deadly

(   ) 13. fearful   M. vast ; huge

(   ) 14. feasible   N. tired ; beat

(   ) 15. feeble   O. frail ; weak

Vocabulary Ratings

5–7 *Good*   8–11 *Very Good*   12–15 *Excellent*

·Synonyms·

1. economical
   = frugal = thrifty

2. extensive
   = wide-ranging
   = widespread

3. enormous
   = vast = huge
   = massive

4. feasible
   = practicable

5. fatal = deadly
   = mortal

6. exceptional
   = extraordinary
   = unusual

7. feeble
   = frail = weak

8. equivalent
   = equal

9. energetic
   = vigorous
   = dynamic

10. exhausted
    = tired = beat
    = worn out

11. faithful
    = loyal
    = devoted

12. engrossed
    = absorbed
    = immersed

13. fantastic
    = terrific
    = excellent

14. ethnic
    = racial

15. fearful
    = scared
    = afraid

fragile 〔'frædʒəl〕 *adj.* 易碎的

Be careful; the old glass is very *fragile*.

（84 交大，82 淡江）

fragrant 〔'fregrənt〕 *adj.* 芳香的

I love roses because they are so *fragrant*.

（87 淡江）

frugal 〔'frugḷ〕 *adj.* 節儉的

Jill was able to save enough money to buy a car by being *frugal* with her daily expenses.

（87 台北大、淡江）

fruitful 〔'frutfəl〕 *adj.* 有收穫的

The meeting was very *fruitful* and now we have a plan of action. （85 中興）

G g

gigantic 〔 dʒaɪˈgæntɪk 〕 *adj.* 巨大的

There is a *gigantic* old tree in front of the house. (84 成大)

global 〔ˈglobḷ 〕 *adj.* 全球的

With the advances in communication, the world has become a *global* village. (88 政大)

gloomy 〔ˈglumɪ 〕 *adj.* 陰暗的

The house is so *gloomy* when the curtains are closed. (86 輔大)

gorgeous 〔ˈgɔrdʒəs 〕 *adj.* 美麗的

The garden looks *gorgeous* when the flowers are in bloom. (85 中興)

gracious (ˈgreʃəs) *adj.* 親切的

She is a *gracious* hostess who always makes her guests feel welcome.

（87 中興，86 輔大）

grac	+ ious
please	+ *adj.*

gradual (ˈgrædʒʊəl) *adj.* 逐漸的

The change of the school was *gradual* but it looks completely different now. （84 淡江）

greedy (ˈgridɪ) *adj.* 貪心的

The *greedy* boy wished to grab all the candy in the jar. （82 交大）

H h

handicapped (ˈhændɪ͵kæpt) *adj.* 殘障的

There are now many special programs and opportunities for the *handicapped*. （85 銘傳）

handy 〔'hændɪ〕 *adj.* 便利的

Your cell phone is a *handy* place to store all of your friends' telephone numbers. (84 成大)

harmonious 〔hɑr'monɪəs〕 *adj.* 和諧的

The man is deeply impressed by the *harmonious* atmosphere of the family he is visiting. (82 交大，80 東吳)

harsh 〔hɑrʃ〕 *adj.* 嚴酷的

Harsh arctic and desert environments have always posed great challenges to human life.

(86 銘傳，81 淡江)

hilarious 〔hə'lɛrɪəs〕 *adj.* 可笑的

The *hilarious* television show made us all laugh. (86 台大)

humble 〔'hʌmbḷ〕 *adj.* 謙虛的

We all think you should not be so *humble*
when you talk to people.

（82 清大，80 中興）

hum	+	ble
ground	+	adj.

humid 〔'hjumɪd〕 *adj.* 潮濕的

The climate of Taiwan is much more *humid*
than that of Alaska. （86 逢甲，85 交大，81 政大，80 逢甲）

hygienic 〔ˌhaɪdʒɪ'ɛnɪk〕 *adj.* 衛生的

This restaurant has been inspected so we
know the food here is *hygienic*. （86 清大）

I i

identical 〔aɪ'dɛntɪkḷ〕 *adj.* 完全相同的

These two shirts look *identical*, and yet
their prices are different. （86 中原、逢甲）

ignorant 〔ˈɪgnərənt 〕 *adj.* 無知的

She was considered *ignorant* because she
had not even finished elementary school.

（84 中興）

i	+ gnor	+ ant
not	+ *know*	+ *adj.*

illegal 〔 ɪˈligḷ 〕 *adj.* 非法的

It is *illegal* to own a gun in our country.

（81 逢甲）

illegible 〔 ɪˈlɛdʒəbḷ 〕 *adj.* 難以辨識的

Mark's handwriting is so *illegible* that I
cannot read his letter. （87、86 中央，85 台大）

illiterate 〔 ɪˈlɪtərɪt 〕 *adj.* 不識字的

The woman asked me to read the letter for
her because she is
illiterate. （86 中正）

il	+ liter	+ ate
not	+ *letter*	+ *adj.*

·Check List·

( ) 1. fragrant	A. aromatic
( ) 2. fruitful	B. agreeable
( ) 3. gigantic	C. modest
( ) 4. global	D. worldwide
( ) 5. gloomy	E. severe ; bitter
( ) 6. gorgeous	F. kind ; amiable
( ) 7. gracious	G. unlawful
( ) 8. harmonious	H. dark ; overcast
( ) 9. harsh	I. uneducated
( ) 10. hilarious	J. titanic ; huge
( ) 11. humble	K. attractive
( ) 12. hygienic	L. sanitary ; clean
( ) 13. illegal	M. unreadable
( ) 14. illegible	N. funny
( ) 15. illiterate	O. rewarding

Vocabulary Ratings

5–7 *Good*   8–11 *Very Good*   12–15 *Excellent*

·Synonyms·

1. fragrant
   = aromatic
   = sweet-smelling

2. illiterate
   = uneducated

3. gigantic
   = titanic = huge
   = enormous

4. illegible
   = unreadable

5. global
   = worldwide

6. gracious
   = kind = amiable

7. humble
   = modest

8. harmonious
   = agreeable

9. harsh
   = severe
   = bitter

10. hilarious
    = funny

11. gorgeous
    = attractive
    = beautiful

12. hygienic
    = sanitary
    = clean

13. illegal
    = unlawful
    = illicit

14. gloomy
    = dark = dim
    = overcast

15. fruitful
    = rewarding

imaginary 〔 ɪˈmædʒəˌnɛrɪ 〕 *adj.* 想像中的

The equator is an *imaginary* circle around the earth. (88中央)

immortal 〔 ɪˈmɔrtḷ 〕 *adj.* 不朽的

Man will die but the spirit is *immortal*.

(87中央)

im	+	mort	+	al
not	+	*death*	+	*adj.*

immune 〔 ɪˈmjun 〕 *adj.* 免疫的

Once you have measles, you will be *immune* to it the rest of your life. (88、87中央)

impartial 〔 ɪmˈparʃəl 〕 *adj.* 公平的

A judge should be *impartial*, not favoring either party. (90台大)

improper 〔 ɪmˈprapɚ 〕 *adj.* 不適當的

Red flowers are *improper* for a funeral.

(85私醫)

impulsive 〔 ɪm'pʌlsɪv 〕 *adj.* 衝動的

He acted without thinking, and now he regrets his *impulsive* act. (88 銘傳，81 中興)

im	+ puls	+ ive
in	+ drive	+ adj.

incompatible 〔 ͵ɪnkəm'pætəbḷ 〕 *adj.*
不合的

The couple often quarreled and finally divorced because they were *incompatible*.

(82 交大，81 中興)

incredible 〔 ɪn'krɛdəbḷ 〕 *adj.* 難以置信的

Einstein's theory of relativity seemed *incredible* when he first introduced it.

(85 私醫，84 清大)

in	+ credi	+ ble
not	+ believe	+ adj.

independent 〔͵ɪndɪˈpɛndənt 〕 *adj.* 獨立的

He works very hard so as to be *independent* of his family. (85 東吳)

indifferent 〔 ɪnˈdɪfərənt 〕 *adj.* 漠不關心的

Baseball fans will never be *indifferent* to the Olympic Baseball Game.

(86 政大、中興，85 私醫，81 政大)

indispensable 〔͵ɪndɪˈspɛnsəbḷ 〕 *adj.* 不可或缺的

Air, food and water are *indispensable* to life; no creature can live without them.

(88 銘傳，86 中興，82 文化，80 淡江)

individual 〔͵ɪndəˈvɪdʒʊəl 〕 *adj.* 獨特的

His work is so original; it is obvious he has an *individual* way of thinking. (85 逢甲)

indulgent 〔 ɪnˈdʌldʒənt 〕 *adj.* 溺愛的

They are such *indulgent* parents that they give their children whatever they want. (82文化)

inevitable 〔 ɪnˈɛvətəbḷ 〕 *adj.* 無法避免的

A fight is *inevitable* because they always disagree and neither gives in.

(88台大)

in	+	evit	+	able
not	+	avoid	+	adj.

inferior 〔 ɪnˈfɪrɪə 〕 *adj.* 較差的

Don't feel *inferior* to others. You should work hard to improve yourself. (87文化)

infinite 〔 ˈɪnfənɪt 〕 *adj.* 無限的

There are an *infinite* number of stars in the universe. (89輔大，86成大)

in	+	fin	+	ite
not	+	end	+	adj.

informative 〔 ɪnˈfɔrmətɪv 〕 *adj.* 知識性的

The lecture was very *informative* and we all learned a lot. (86 私醫)

inherent 〔 ɪnˈhɪrənt 〕 *adj.* 天生的

The instinct for survival seems to be *inherent* in human beings.

(82 文化)

in	+	her	+ ent
in	+	heir	+ adj.

innate 〔 ɪˈnet 〕 *adj.* 天生的

Man's ability to walk on two legs is *innate*.

(85 逢甲)

innocent 〔 ˈɪnəsn̩t 〕 *adj.* 無辜的

The boy claimed that he was *innocent*. He said that he didn't steal the money from the store. (87 東吳)

in	+	noc	+ ent
not	+	harm	+ adj.

innumerable 〔 ɪ'njumərəbḷ 〕 *adj.* 無數的

There are *innumerable* fish in the seas. (82 文化)

instant 〔'ɪnstənt 〕 *adj.* 立即的

The book was an *instant* best seller, and the
author became famous overnight. (86 交大)

instinctive 〔 ɪn'stɪŋktɪv 〕 *adj.* 本能的

It is *instinctive* that a man will close his eyes
when he sees strong light. (87 中原,82 文化)

intact 〔 ɪn'tækt 〕 *adj.* 完整的

The storm ravaged nearly the whole village,
but their house remained *intact*.

(86 銘傳,82 文化,80 淡江)

in + tact
 | |
not + *touch*

integral 〔'ɪntəgrəl 〕 *adj.* 必要的

The windows and the doors are *integral*
parts of a house. (82 文化)

·Check List·

(   ) 1. immortal   A. self-reliant

(   ) 2. impartial   B. endless

(   ) 3. incompatible   C. distinctive

(   ) 4. incredible   D. essential

(   ) 5. independent   E. countless

(   ) 6. indifferent   F. innate

(   ) 7. indispensable   G. unbelievable

(   ) 8. individual   H. eternal

(   ) 9. inevitable   I. whole

(   ) 10. infinite   J. discordant

(   ) 11. informative   K. unavoidable

(   ) 12. inherent   L. educational

(   ) 13. innumerable   M. fair

(   ) 14. instant   N. uninterested

(   ) 15. intact   O. immediate

Vocabulary Ratings

5–7 *Good*   8–11 *Very Good*   12–15 *Excellent*

• Synonyms •

1. immortal
   = eternal
   = everlasting

2. impartial
   = fair

3. incompatible
   = discordant

4. incredible
   = unbelievable

5. independent
   = self-reliant

6. indifferent
   = uninterested
   = uncaring

7. indispensable
   = essential
   = vital

8. innumerable
   = countless

9. individual
   = distinctive
   = unique

10. inevitable
    = unavoidable

11. infinite
    = endless
    = boundless

12. informative
    = educational
    = instructive

13. inherent
    = innate
    = instinctive

14. instant
    = immediate
    = prompt

15. intact
    = whole

intellectual 〔͵ɪntl̩ˈɛktʃʊəl 〕 *adj.* 智力的

Nutrition is important for children's *intellectual* development. （80淡江）

intense 〔 ɪnˈtɛns 〕 *adj.* 強烈的

The *intense* heat makes everyone uncomfortable. （86銘傳）

internal 〔 ɪnˈtɝnl̩ 〕 *adj.* 內部的

The X-ray showed the doctor a clear picture of the patient's *internal* organs. （85逢甲）

intimate 〔ˈɪntəmɪt 〕 *adj.* 親密的

We are *intimate* friends. We can share everything with each other. （86輔大，81中興，80文化）

invalid 〔 ɪnˈvælɪd 〕 *adj.* 無效的

Your license has expired; it is *invalid* now.

（81台大）

in	+	val	+	id
not	+	*strong*	+	*adj.*

irrational 〔 ɪ'ræʃən! 〕 *adj.* 不理性的

Stop being so *irrational*. You are acting
like a child. (80中興)

ir	+	ration	+	al
not	+	*reason*	+	*adj.*

irrelevant 〔 ɪ'rɛləvənt 〕 *adj.* 無關的

What she says now is *irrelevant* because we
have already made our decision. (80中興，淡江)

J j

juvenile 〔'dʒuvən! 〕 *adj.* 少年的

In some libraries young people can check
out ten *juvenile* books at
one time. (87中興)

juven	+	ile
young	+	*adj.*

K k

keen 〔 kin 〕 *adj.* 敏銳的

The scientist has a *keen* mind and is able to
solve complicated problems. (86逢甲)

knowledgeable (ˈnɑlɪdʒəbḷ) *adj.* 學識
豐富的

Mr. Williams is a very *knowledgeable*
person in this field. (85 東吳)

L l

legitimate (lɪˈdʒɪtəmɪt) *adj.* 合法的

He was judged to be the *legitimate* owner
of the property. (86 銘傳)

logical (ˈlɑdʒɪkḷ) *adj.* 合邏輯的

Your argument is not *logical* at all. It
doesn't make any sense. (81 中興)

luxurious (lʌgˈʒʊrɪəs) *adj.* 豪華的

To a beggar a lush carpet of pine needles
is more welcome than the most *luxurious*
Persian rug. (82 政大)

M m

mandatory 〔'mændə,torɪ〕 *adj.* 必要的

In Taiwan, it is *mandatory* for every child
to attend school
until he is 16.

（85 文化，81 政大）

```
manda + tory
  |        |
order  +  adj.
```

marine 〔mə'rin〕 *adj.* 海洋的

Marine plants can grow in salt water. （85 輔大）

mature 〔mə'tjʊr〕 *adj.* 成熟的

Years later, May has grown up to be a
mature and elegant lady. （86 銘傳，85 逢甲，83 淡江）

medieval 〔,midɪ'ivḷ〕 *adj.* 中世紀的

"The *medieval* times" is also called "the
Dark Ages." （85 輔大）

```
medi + eval
  |      |
middle + age
```

melancholy 〔'mɛlən,kɑlɪ〕 *adj.* 憂鬱的

The *melancholy* music makes me feel sad.

（86 輔大）

```
melan  +  chol        +  y
  |        |              |
black  +  bile (膽汁) + adj.
（從前人們認為體內黑膽汁較多，會使人憂鬱）
```

memorial 〔mə'morɪəl〕 *adj.* 紀念的

They built a *memorial* hall to honor President Lincoln. （85 淡江）

mental 〔'mɛntl̩〕 *adj.* 心理的

Although he has great *mental* powers, he is not strong physically. （80 淡江）

miraculous 〔mə'rækjələs〕 *adj.* 奇蹟般的

The boy's recovery from the disease was considered *miraculous* because no one had expected him to survive. （88 中正，82 文化）

miserable 〔'mɪzərəbḷ〕 *adj.* 悲慘的

The child is cold, hungry and tired, so of course he is feeling *miserable*. (82 政大)

moderate 〔'mɑdərɪt〕 *adj.* 節制的

You should be *moderate* in drinking, eating and spending. (87 淡江)

moist 〔 mɔɪst 〕 *adj.* 潮濕的

Tea grows best in a cool, *moist* climate.

(84 成大,82 私醫,80 逢甲)

moral 〔'mɔrəl〕 *adj.* 道德的

Parents try to instill *moral* concepts in their children by teaching them what is right and wrong. (87 中興,86 逢甲)

·Check List·

(   )   1. intense   A.   legal

(   )   2. intimate   B.   powerful

(   )   3. invalid   C.   compulsory

(   )   4. irrational   D.   gloomy

(   )   5. irrelevant   E.   temperate

(   )   6. keen   F.   unreasonable

(   )   7. knowledgeable   G.   sharp

(   )   8. legitimate   H.   ethical

(   )   9. logical   I.   close

(   ) 10. mandatory   J.   wretched

(   ) 11. mature   K.   unrelated

(   ) 12. melancholy   L.   rational

(   ) 13. miserable   M.   void

(   ) 14. moderate   N.   full-grown

(   ) 15. moral   O.   well-informed

Vocabulary Ratings

5–7 *Good*   8–11 *Very Good*   12–15 *Excellent*

·Synonyms·

1. intense
   = powerful
   = severe

2. intimate
   = close

3. mature
   = full-grown

4. irrational
   = unreasonable
   = senseless

5. irrelevant
   = unrelated

6. mandatory
   = compulsory
   = obligatory

7. knowledgeable
   = well-informed

8. legitimate
   = legal = lawful

9. logical
   = rational
   = reasonable

10. keen
    = sharp
    = acute

11. invalid
    = void
    = illegal

12. melancholy
    = gloomy
    = dismal

13. miserable
    = wretched

14. moderate
    = temperate
    = restrained

15. moral
    = ethical

multiple 〔ˈmʌltəpḷ〕 *adj.* 多重的

There are *multiple* benefits to a university education.（輔大）

multi	+	ple
many	+	*fold*

mutual 〔ˈmjutʃʊəl〕 *adj.* 彼此的

They often quarrel for lack of *mutual* understanding.（88 中正，87 中央）

N n

naïve 〔nɑˈiv〕 *adj.* 天眞的

Because he was *naïve* about business, the salesman was able to take advantage of him.

（85 逢甲）

naked 〔ˈnekɪd〕 *adj.* 赤裸的

A virus is so small that it cannot be seen by the *naked* eye.（85 政大）

nimble 〔ˈnɪmbḷ〕 *adj.* 敏捷的

The *nimble* policeman leaped over the fence to pursue the car thief. (81 台大，80 淡江)

notorious 〔noˈtorɪəs〕 *adj.* 惡名昭彰的

Despite his *notorious* arrogance, I felt I could do business with him. (84 台北大，82 政大)

nuclear 〔ˈnjuklɪɚ〕 *adj.* 核子的

Some people oppose developing *nuclear* weapons because they are too destructive.

(81 逢甲)

nutritious 〔njuˈtrɪʃəs〕 *adj.* 營養的

Whole wheat bread is considered *nutritious* and healthful. (88 銘傳)

nutri	+ tious
nourish（滋養）+	*adj.*

O o

objective 〔 əb'dʒɛktɪv 〕 *adj.* 客觀的

Newspaper articles should be as *objective* as possible. (86 逢甲)

optimistic 〔 ͵ɑptə'mɪstɪk 〕 *adj.* 樂觀的

Carl's outlook is *optimistic*. (88 中央，84 交大)

optional 〔 'ɑpʃənḷ 〕 *adj.* 可選擇的

The art class is *optional*, but all students must take mathematics.

(88 政大，85 逢甲)

opt	+	ion	+	al
wish	+	*n.*	+	*adj.*

outdated 〔 aut'detɪd 〕 *adj.* 過時的

Some people say typewriters are *outdated* machines that have been replaced by computers. (86 銘傳)

outstanding 〔aʊtˈstændɪŋ〕 *adj.* 傑出的

The band gave an *outstanding* performance and the audience clapped enthusiastically.

（86 中興）

overcrowded 〔ˌovɚˈkraʊdɪd〕 *adj.* 過度擁擠的

John tried to get on the bus, but it was already *overcrowded*. （84 私醫）

overwhelming 〔ˌovɚˈhwɛlmɪŋ〕 *adj.* 壓倒性的

The party won an *overwhelming* victory in the general election. （85 台大，81 交大）

P p

panicked 〔ˈpænɪkt〕 *adj.* 驚慌的

The crowd became *panicked* when someone shouted "Fire." （85 台大）

partial ﹝'parʃəl﹞ adj. 部分的

What we heard was a *partial* report of the meeting. (87輔大，86中興)

pathetic ﹝pə'θɛtɪk﹞ adj. 可憐的

We could not help but feel sorry for the *pathetic* stray dog. (86台大，80淡江)

pathe + tic	patri + otic
| |	| |
suffer + *adj.*	*father* + *adj.*

patriotic ﹝͵petrɪ'atɪk﹞ adj. 愛國的

Thousands of *patriotic* students were killed by ruthless soldiers in Tienanmen Square. (80文化)

peculiar ﹝pɪ'kjulɪɚ﹞ adj. 奇特的

Children often say *peculiar* things. (82清大)

peerless 〔'pɪrlɪs 〕 *adj.* 無與倫比的

The masterpiece is a *peerless* work of art, so it is impossible to compare it to anything else. (81 中興)

perceptible 〔 pəˈsɛptəbḷ 〕 *adj.* 看得見的

The outline of the figure was barely *perceptible* in the darkness. (85 台大)

permanent 〔'pɝmənənt 〕 *adj.* 永久的

After a series of temporary jobs, John found a *permanent* position in a big company.

(82 淡江)

perpetual 〔 pəˈpɛtʃuəl 〕 *adj.* 永久的

The *perpetual* motion of the earth as it turns on its axis creates the change of seasons.

(85 銘傳)

per	+ pet	+ ual
throughout	+ seek	+ adj.

Check List

( ) 1. multiple   A. innocent

( ) 2. naïve   B. unequaled

( ) 3. naked   C. irresistible

( ) 4. notorious   D. obsolete

( ) 5. nutritious   E. bare

( ) 6. optimistic   F. frightened

( ) 7. optional   G. nourishing

( ) 8. outdated   H. manifold

( ) 9. outstanding   I. visible

( ) 10. overwhelming   J. perpetual

( ) 11. panicked   K. infamous

( ) 12. pathetic   L. elective

( ) 13. peerless   M. remarkable

( ) 14. perceptible   N. positive

( ) 15. permanent   O. pitiful

Vocabulary Ratings

5–7 *Good*   8–11 *Very Good*   12–15 *Excellent*

·Synonyms·

1. naked
   = bare

2. peerless
   = unequaled
   = unrivaled

3. nutritious
   = nourishing
   = wholesome

4. optimistic
   = positive
   = hopeful

5. outdated
   = obsolete
   = out-of-date
   = old-fashioned

6. outstanding
   = remarkable
   = excellent

7. overwhelming
   = irresistible

8. panicked
   = frightened
   = panicky

9. multiply
   = manifold

10. pathetic
    = pitiful

11. naïve
    = innocent
    = childlike

12. notorious
    = infamous

13. optional
    = elective

14. perceptible
    = visible

15. permanent
    = perpetual
    = eternal

perplexed 〔 pɚ'plɛkst 〕 *adj.* 困惑的

Tom's *perplexed* expression showed that he did not understand what his teacher was saying. (87 清大)

pessimistic 〔 ˌpɛsə'mɪstɪk 〕 *adj.* 悲觀的

A *pessimistic* person always assumes that the worst will happen. (88 中央, 86 輔大)

pious 〔 'paɪəs 〕 *adj.* 虔誠的

My uncle is a very *pious* man and goes to church every Sunday. (86 清大)

pitiful 〔 'pɪtɪfəl 〕 *adj.* 可憐的

The man told us a *pitiful* story that touched us deeply. (86 台大, 80 淡江)

plentiful 〔'plɛntɪfəl 〕 adj. 豐富的

The farmers celebrated the *plentiful* harvest.

（89 輔大，84 交大）

plenti	+	ful
|		|
fill	+	*adj.*

port	+	able
|		|
carry	+	*adj.*

portable 〔'portəbḷ 〕 adj. 手提的

We carried a *portable* stereo with us when we went on a picnic last Sunday. （80 淡江）

potent 〔'potn̩t 〕 adj. 有效的

This medicine is very *potent*, so you only need to take a little. （86 成大）

preceding 〔 prɪ'sidɪŋ 〕 adj. 在前的

The question has been mentioned in the *preceding* chapter.

（84 淡江）

pre	+	ced	+	ing
|		|		|
before	+	*go*	+	*adj.*

precise 〔 prɪ'saɪs 〕 *adj.* 準確的

The *precise* time of the meeting will be 2:15. Please don't be late. (87中央，84交大)

pregnant 〔'prɛgnənt 〕 *adj.* 懷孕的

The *pregnant* woman said that she would soon have twins. (83淡江)

pressing 〔'prɛsɪŋ 〕 *adj.* 迫切的

The most *pressing* problem any economic system faces is how to use its scarce resources. (86中原)

previous 〔'privɪəs 〕 *adj.* 先前的

My *previous* job gave me a lot of training in computer programming. (84文化)

pre	+	vi	+	ous
before	+	way	+	adj.

primary （'praɪˌmɛrɪ）*adj.* 主要的

Do not lose sight of your *primary* objectives.

（83 文化，81 台大）

```
prim + ary
  |     |
first + adj.
```

prime 〔 praɪm 〕*adj.* 最好的

The successful sitcom <u>Three's Company</u>
was shown during *prime* time on TV.

（86 銘傳，84 成大）

primitive 〔'prɪmətɪv〕*adj.* 原始的

Primitive man used fire to drive away
dangerous animals. （81 台大）

prior 〔'praɪə〕*adj.* 在～之前

Prior to the use of computers, there was a
big waste of human resources. （84 交大，82 私醫）

professional 〔 prəˈfɛʃənḷ 〕 *adj.* 專業的

When I asked the lawyer about my case, he gave me his *professional* advice. (85 銘傳)

proficient 〔 prəˈfɪʃənt 〕 *adj.* 熟練的

By practicing hard every day, he became *proficient* with his violin. (87 政大)

pro	+ fic	+ ient
|	|	|
forward	+ *do*	+ *adj.*

profitable 〔ˈprɑfɪtəbḷ〕 *adj.* 賺錢的

The restaurant was not *profitable* because there were not enough customers. (87 台大)

profound 〔 prəˈfaʊnd 〕 *adj.* 深的

The man expressed his *profound* gratitude when I returned his wallet. (82 文化)

prosperous 〔'prɑspərəs 〕 *adj.* 興盛的

The *prosperous* company makes a lot of money for its owners. (89 輔大,86 中正)

provocative 〔 prə'vɑkətɪv 〕 *adj.* 挑釁的

He made a *provocative* remark because he wanted to start an argument. (86 政大)

pro	+ voc	+ ative
|	|	|
forth	+ *call*	+ *adj.*

punctual 〔'pʌŋktʃuəl 〕 *adj.* 準時的

Professor Chang is *punctual*; he is never late. (84 交大)

puzzling 〔'pʌzl̩ɪŋ 〕 *adj.* 令人困惑的

The question he raised was so *puzzling* that neither of us knew how to answer it.

(86 中正、中原)

·Check List·

(   )   1. perplexed   A. effective

(   )   2. pious   B. principal

(   )   3. pitiful   C. specialized

(   )   4. potent   D. challenging

(   )   5. preceding   E. puzzled

(   )   6. pressing   F. lucrative

(   )   7. primary   G. urgent

(   )   8. prime   H. prompt

(   )   9. primitive   I. aboriginal

(   ) 10. professional   J. devout

(   ) 11. proficient   K. deep

(   ) 12. profitable   L. pathetic

(   ) 13. profound   M. adept

(   ) 14. provocative   N. previous

(   ) 15. punctual   O. best

Vocabulary Ratings

5–7 *Good*   8–11 *Very Good*   12–15 *Excellent*

·Synonyms·

1. perplexed
   = puzzled
   = bewildered
   = baffled
   = confused

2. pious
   = devout
   = religious

3. pitiful
   = pathetic
   = miserable

4. primary
   = principal
   = chief

5. preceding
   = previous
   = former

6. profitable
   = lucrative

7. profound
   = deep

8. pressing
   = urgent
   = crucial

9. potent
   = effective

10. prime
    = best

11. primitive
    = aboriginal

12. professional
    = specialized
    = expert

13. proficient
    = adept
    = skilled

14. provocative
    = challenging

15. punctual
    = prompt
    = on time

Q q

qualified 〔'kwɑlə,faɪd〕 *adj.* 合格的

He is not *qualified* to teach English.

（81 交大，80 輔大）

R r

radiant 〔'redɪənt〕 *adj.* 容光煥發的

She was *radiant* with joy at her wedding.

（85 清大）

radi	+ ant
ray（光線）	+ *adj.*

random 〔'rændəm〕 *adj.* 隨意的

She opened the telephone book, chose a *random* number and dialed the number for fun.（87 中興、中正）

refreshing 〔rɪ'frɛʃɪŋ〕 *adj.* 清爽的

In the middle of the desert, they found a *refreshing* spring.（82 交大）

relevant (ˈrɛləvənt) *adj.* 有關的

My teacher told me to take out the last
paragraph of my essay because it was not
relevant to the topic. (86 政大、中正)

reliable (rɪˈlaɪəbḷ) *adj.* 可靠的

I want to buy a *reliable* car so that I don't
have to spend a lot of money on repairs.

(89 成大，88 中正，85 台大，86 輔大)

reluctant (rɪˈlʌktənt) *adj.* 不願意的

She was *reluctant* to go with him, so she
tried to make up an excuse.

(84 台北大，81 交大，79 中興)

remarkable (rɪˈmɑrkəbḷ) *adj.* 出色的

He is really a *remarkable* baseball player
and stands out from the rest of the team.

(81 淡江)

renowned 〔 rɪˋnaʊnd 〕 *adj.* 有名的

A *renowned* scientist was invited to deliver a lecture at our school. (輔大)

re	+ nown	+ ed
again	+ *name*	+ *adj.*

required 〔 rɪˋkwaɪrd 〕 *adj.* 必修的

English is a *required* subject for all high school students in Taiwan. (85文化)

resistant 〔 rɪˋzɪstənt 〕 *adj.* 抵抗的

With a healthy diet, the body becomes *resistant* to disease. (88中正，86交大)

re	+ sist	+ ant
back	+ *stand*	+ *adj.*

respectable 〔rɪ'spɛktəbḷ〕 *adj.* 可敬的

Old John is poor but *respectable*. （86輔大）

re	+ spect	+ able
|	|	|
again +	*see* +	*adj.*

respective 〔rɪ'spɛktɪv〕 *adj.* 個別的

There are three children in my family and
and we have our *respective* rooms. （82台大）

ridiculous 〔rɪ'dɪkjələs〕 *adj.* 荒謬的

Fred's claim that he can run a mile in four
minutes is simply *ridiculous*.

（86成大，82交大，80清大）

rough 〔rʌf〕 *adj.* 粗糙的

The carpenter sanded the *rough* wood in
order to make it smooth. （86中興）

routine 〔 ru'tin 〕 *adj.* 例行的

Don't worry. This is just a *routine* physical examination. (85 淡江)

rude 〔 rud 〕 *adj.* 無禮的

The clerk was *rude* to his superior too often; now he is out of work. (87 逢甲，81 淡江)

ruthless 〔'ruθlɪs 〕 *adj.* 無情的

The *ruthless* father turned his son away from home. (87 逢甲)

S s

savage 〔'sævɪdʒ 〕 *adj.* 野蠻的

The early settlers of America considered native Americans *savage* people. (85 清大)

sensitive 〔'sɛnsətɪv 〕 *adj.* 敏感的

The photographic paper is *sensitive* to light; once exposed, the paper changes color. (85 淡江)

severe 〔 sə'vɪr 〕 *adj.* 嚴厲的

Because he made a serious mistake, his father gave him a *severe* punishment. (86 中興、銘傳)

shallow 〔 'ʃælo 〕 *adj.* 淺的

We can walk across the river here because the water is *shallow*. (82 淡江)

sincere 〔 sɪn'sɪr 〕 *adj.* 誠懇的

In this letter, I express my *sincere* sympathy for your loss. (87 政大，86 中興)

skeptical 〔 'skɛptɪkl̩ 〕 *adj.* 懷疑的

Though the evidence was overwhelming, one juror was still *skeptical*. (86 中興，85 銘傳)

slender 〔 'slɛndɚ 〕 *adj.* 苗條的

Betty wishes she could be as *slender* as Margaret. (86 輔大，84 淡江)

·Check List·

(   ) 1. qualified   A. dependable

(   ) 2. radiant   B. individual

(   ) 3. random   C. offensive

(   ) 4. relevant   D. harsh ; strict

(   ) 5. reliable   E. outstanding

(   ) 6. reluctant   F. casual

(   ) 7. remarkable   G. merciless

(   ) 8. respective   H. earnest

(   ) 9. rough   I. eligible

(   ) 10. rude   J. coarse

(   ) 11. ruthless   K. unwilling

(   ) 12. severe   L. slim ; trim

(   ) 13. sincere   M. glowing

(   ) 14. skeptical   N. suspicious

(   ) 15. slender   O. connected

Vocabulary Ratings

5–7 *Good*   8–11 *Very Good*   12–15 *Excellent*

·Synonyms·

1. qualified
   = eligible

2. radiant
   = glowing
   = beaming

3. random
   = casual

4. relevant
   = connected
   = related

5. reliable
   = dependable

6. rough
   = coarse

7. remarkable
   = outstanding
   = amazing

8. respective
   = individual

9. reluctant
   = unwilling
   = hesitant

10. rude
    = offensive
    = impolite

11. ruthless
    = merciless
    = cruel

12. severe
    = harsh = strict
    = stern

13. sincere
    = earnest
    = heartfelt

14. skeptical
    = suspicious
    = doubtful

15. slender
    = slim = trim

slight 〔 slaɪt 〕 *adj.* 輕微的

I'm not really ill, but I have a *slight* headache. (86台大)

slippery 〔'slɪpərɪ 〕 *adj.* 滑的

After the rain, the sidewalk becomes *slippery*. You had better watch your step.

(86台大)

sluggish 〔'slʌgɪʃ 〕 *adj.* 遲緩的

Cold-blooded animals are *sluggish* in extremely cold weather.

(89輔大，80淡江)

```
slug + gish
  |      |
slow  +  adj.
```

solar 〔'solɚ 〕 *adj.* 太陽的

There is a huge *solar*-heated swimming pool in our community. (83逢甲)

solemn 〔ˈsɑləm 〕 *adj.* 莊嚴的

A funeral is a *solemn* occasion; it is not
appropriate to make jokes. (86 中興)

solid 〔ˈsɑlɪd 〕 *adj.* 堅固的

A *solid* foundation is required before
building a skyscraper. (86 輔大、中原)

sophisticated 〔 səˈfɪstɪˌketɪd 〕 *adj.*
複雜的

The machine is *sophisticated*. I can't
operate it without the manual. (88 台大、中央)

spacious 〔ˈspeʃəs 〕 *adj.* 寬敞的

The director's *spacious* new office
overlooked the city. (88 銘傳，86 輔大)

spontaneous ﹝ spɑn'tenɪəs ﹞ *adj.* 自動自發的

The audience burst into *spontaneous* applause when the singer appeared.

（90、81台大）

stable ﹝'stebḷ﹞ *adj.* 穩定的

The more *stable* a society's economic situation is, the more *stable* the society will be.（84交大，82東吳）

stingy ﹝'stɪndʒɪ﹞ *adj.* 吝嗇的

He is very *stingy*; never expect him to give a cent to a beggar.（86台大）

strenuous ﹝'strɛnjuəs﹞ *adj.* 費力的

The hike up the mountain was *strenuous*.

（80淡江，東吳）

strict 〔 strɪkt 〕 *adj.* 嚴格的

Psychologists have found that *strict* regulations do not always make a child more well-behaved. (89 輔大，86 台大，85 文化)

stubborn 〔'stʌbən 〕 *adj.* 固執的

The child is too *stubborn* to be reasoned with. (87 中興)

sturdy 〔'stɜdɪ 〕 *adj.* 健壯的

The little boy grew strong and *sturdy* under the care of his mother. (86 輔大、中原)

subjective 〔 səb'dʒɛktɪv 〕 *adj.* 主觀的

Your statement is *subjective*; it is based on opinion, not fact. (86 逢甲)

subtle 〔'sʌtḷ 〕 *adj.* 細微的

He made a *subtle* observation of the changes and recorded it in his report. (82 文化)

suburban 〔 səˈbɝbən 〕 *adj.* 郊區的

More and more people move into *suburban* areas not far from major cities. (83 交大)

```
sub + urb + an
 |     |    |
near + city + adj.
```

```
suf + fic + ient
 |     |     |
over + do  + adj.
```

sufficient 〔 səˈfɪʃənt 〕 *adj.* 足夠的

This nation has a reserve of oil *sufficient* for its needs. (88 政大，87 淡江)

superficial 〔 ˌsupɚˈfɪʃəl 〕 *adj.* 表面的

Not being interested in the subject, he only gained a *superficial* knowledge of it. (82 文化)

superior 〔 səˈpɪrɪɚ 〕 *adj.* 優越的

They consider themselves the most *superior* race in the world. (87 中興，80 淡江)

swift 〔 swɪft 〕 *adj.* 快速的

The *swift* current of the river carried us downstream quickly. (84 成大)

sympathetic 〔ˌsɪmpəˈθɛtɪk 〕 *adj.* 同情的

I gave her a *sympathetic* look to show that I understood her situation. (88 中央，85 台大)

synthetic 〔 sɪnˈθɛtɪk 〕 *adj.* 合成的

This *synthetic* fabric is much stronger than cotton or silk.

(85 銘傳)

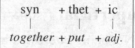

T t

tactful 〔ˈtæktfəl 〕 *adj.* 圓滑的

If you don't want to go, you should be *tactful* and say that you are busy. (86 中興、輔大)

•Check List•

( ) 1. slight   A. firm

( ) 2. sluggish   B. miserly

( ) 3. solid   C. compassionate

( ) 4. spacious   D. surface

( ) 5. stable   E. obstinate

( ) 6. stingy   F. excellent

( ) 7. strenuous   G. minor ; small

( ) 8. stubborn   H. laborious

( ) 9. sturdy   I. steady

( ) 10. sufficient   J. robust ; strong

( ) 11. superficial   K. lethargic

( ) 12. superior   L. rapid ; quick

( ) 13. swift   M. adequate

( ) 14. sympathetic   N. diplomatic

( ) 15. tactful   O. roomy

Vocabulary Ratings

5–7 *Good*   8–11 *Very Good*   12–15 *Excellent*

·Synonyms·

1. slight
   = minor
   = small

2. sluggish
   = lethargic
   = slow

3. solid
   = firm

4. spacious
   = roomy

5. sturdy
   = robust
   = strong

6. swift
   = rapid = fast
   = quick

7. strenuous
   = laborious
   = exhausting

8. stubborn
   = obstinate

9. stable
   = steady
   = unchanging

10. sufficient
    = adequate
    = enough

11. superficial
    = surface
    = skin-deep

12. superior
    = excellent

13. stingy
    = miserly

14. sympathetic
    = compassionate

15. tactful
    = diplomatic

talkative ('tɔkətɪv) *adj.* 愛說話的
Jane is such a *talkative* girl that she always
has something to say. (86輔大)

tame (tem) *adj.* 溫馴的
Domestic animals are usually *tame*. (85輔大)

tardy ('tɑrdɪ) *adj.* 遲緩的
Some professors find that students who are
tardy tend to earn lower grades. (86輔大)

tedious ('tidɪəs) *adj.* 乏味的
The official celebration was an extremely
tedious affair. (84政大)

temperate ('tɛmpərɪt) *adj.* 溫和的
This country has a pleasant, *temperate*
climate — not too hot and not too cold.
(85交大)

temper	+ ate
moderate (調節)	+ *adj.*

tense 〔 tɛns 〕 *adj.* 緊張的

People who are too *tense* tend to have more
health problems than those who are relaxed.

（ 87 逢甲，86 輔大 ）

terrifying 〔'tɛrə,faɪɪŋ 〕 *adj.* 可怕的

We had a *terrifying* experience when the bus
ran off the road.

（ 86 中原 ）

terr	+ ify	+ ing
frighten	+ *v.*	+ *adj.*

thorough 〔'θɜo 〕 *adj.* 徹底的

The police made a *thorough* search for the
escaped criminal, but in vain. （ 81、80 淡江 ）

thrifty 〔'θrɪftɪ 〕 *adj.* 節儉的

A *thrifty* buyer purchases fruits and
vegetables in season. （ 85 銘傳 ）

tidy ('taɪdɪ) *adj.* 整潔的

The students are expected to keep their dormitory room *tidy*. (87 中央，82 私醫，81 淡江)

timid ('tɪmɪd) *adj.* 膽小的

Sherry is a *timid* girl. She is afraid of being alone at home. (81 淡江)

```
 tim + id
  |     |
fear + adj.
```

tiny ('taɪnɪ) *adj.* 微小的

Be careful. There is a *tiny* crack in the plate. (84 成大)

tolerant ('tɑlərənt) *adj.* 容忍的

A man with a big heart is *tolerant* of other people's different opinions. (87 中原，82 文化，80 淡江)

total ('totl̩) *adj.* 完全的

The war ended in *total* victory for the Allies. (81 清大)

toxic 〔'tɑksɪk〕 *adj.* 有毒的

Many people were rushed to the hospital after inhaling the *toxic* gas emitted from the factory.

（89 輔大，86 成大，81 台大）

tox	+	ic
poison	+	adj.

tragic 〔'trædʒɪk〕 *adj.* 悲慘的

The movie told the *tragic* story of the Titanic. （86 台大）

transient 〔'trænʃənt〕 *adj.* 短暫的

Time flies like an arrow. Life is so *transient.* （84 交大）

trans	+ i(t) +	ent
across	+ go +	adj.

trivial 〔'trɪvjəl〕 *adj.* 瑣碎的

Mary always gets upset about *trivial* matters. （85 銘傳，84 政大）

typical 〔'tɪpɪk!〕 *adj.* 典型的

It is *typical* of him to make such sarcastic remarks. (86中原，87、86逢甲)

U u

ultimate 〔'ʌltəmɪt〕 *adj.* 最終的

The *ultimate* purpose of learning is to serve the society. (83淡江)

ultim + ate
| |
last + *adj.*

un + anim + ous
| | |
one + *mind* + *adj.*

unanimous 〔 ju'nænəməs 〕 *adj.* 全體一致的

Scientists are not *unanimous* about the reasons for the extinction of dinosaurs.

(86中興)

unconscious ﹝ ʌnˈkɑnʃəs ﹞ *adj.* 無意識的

He was knocked *unconscious* by a falling rock. (85 銘傳，84 私醫)

understated ﹝ˈʌndɚˈstetɪd ﹞ *adj.* 低調的

Maggie gave a brief and *understated* account of what had happened. (81 中興)

unemployed ﹝ˌʌnɪmˈplɔɪd ﹞ *adj.* 失業的

My brother was laid off last month and is now *unemployed.* (85 銘傳)

unique ﹝ juˈnik ﹞ *adj.* 獨一無二的

Like fingerprints, each person's DNA is *unique.* (88 銘傳，86 中興、逢甲)

universal ﹝ˌjunəˈvɝsḷ ﹞ *adj.* 普遍的

Children's curiosity and energy are *universal.* (88 政大，86 中興)

uni + vers + al
| | |
one + turn + adj.

·Check List·

(   ) 1. tame   A. meek

(   ) 2. tedious   B. stressed

(   ) 3. temperate   C. entire ; whole

(   ) 4. tense   D. temporary

(   ) 5. terrifying   E. neat ; orderly

(   ) 6. thorough   F. undivided

(   ) 7. tidy   G. moderate

(   ) 8. timid   H. frightening

(   ) 9. total   I. poisonous

(   ) 10. toxic   J. jobless

(   ) 11. tragic   K. detailed

(   ) 12. transient   L. petty

(   ) 13. trivial   M. boring ; dull

(   ) 14. unanimous   N. cowardly

(   ) 15. unemployed   O. disastrous

Vocabulary Ratings

5–7 *Good*   8–11 *Very Good*   12–15 *Excellent*

·Synonyms·

1. tame = meek
   = domesticated

2. tedious
   = boring = dull

3. temperate
   = moderate
   = mild

4. tense
   = stressed
   = nervous

5. terrifying
   = frightening
   = dreadful

6. thorough
   = detailed = full

7. tidy = neat
   = orderly

8. toxic
   = poisonous

9. timid
   = cowardly
   = shy

10. total
    = entire
    = whole
    = complete

11. tragic
    = disastrous

12. transient
    = temporary
    = fleeting

13. trivial
    = petty

14. unanimous
    = undivided

15. unemployed
    = jobless
    = out of work

urban 〔ˈɝbən〕 *adj.* 都市的

Many people living in the countryside long for an *urban* life.

（86 逢甲，83 中興）

```
urb  + an
 |      |
city  + adj.
```

urgent 〔ˈɝdʒənt〕 *adj.* 緊急的

He was in *urgent* need of money and thus he turned to Mr. Wang for help. （86 中原）

V v

vacant 〔ˈvekənt〕 *adj.* 空的

Many cars were parked in the *vacant* lot.

（86 銘傳）

```
vac   + ant
 |       |
empty  + adj.
```

vague 〔veg〕 *adj.* 模糊的

They felt that the suggestions were too *vague* to be of much value. （87 中正，82 清大）

valid 〔ˈvælɪd〕 *adj.* 有效的

This ticket is only *valid* for two days. （87 中興）

vast 〔 væst 〕 *adj.* 廣大的

Mass production yields *vast* quantities of goods for domestic and foreign use. （86 銘傳）

verbal 〔ˈvɜbḷ〕 *adj.* 語言的

Teachers have to pay attention to students' *verbal* ability. （87 輔大）

vexed 〔 vɛkst 〕 *adj.* 煩惱的

She was *vexed* when she discovered she had forgotten her key. （86 中正，81 淡江）

vigorous 〔ˈvɪgərəs〕 *adj.* 精力充沛的

Though over 70, Mr. Wilson is still *vigorous* and works out regularly. （80 淡江）

visible 〔'vɪzəbḷ〕 *adj.* 看得見的

In heavy fog, cars going in the opposite direction are hardly *visible*. (87 台大，86 成大)

vis + ible	vit + al
| |	| |
see + adj.	*live + adj.*

vital 〔'vaɪtḷ〕 *adj.* 非常重要的

Your support is *vital* for the success of my project. (86 銘傳，84 逢甲)

vulgar 〔'vʌlgɚ〕 *adj.* 粗俗的

Don't use such *vulgar* words. It is considered impolite. (81 淡江)

vulnerable 〔'vʌlnərəbḷ〕 *adj.* 易受傷的

Young people are *vulnerable* to the influence of television. (87 中興)

W w

weary 〔'wɪrɪ〕 *adj.* 疲倦的

In a desert an oasis is a welcome relief to
weary travelers. (87 逢甲，82 私醫)

wholesome 〔'holsəm〕 *adj.* 有益健康的

Natural food is *wholesome* for health. (81 淡江)

wicked 〔'wɪkɪd〕 *adj.* 邪惡的

The *wicked* witch turned the prince into an
ugly frog. (82 逢甲)

worthwhile 〔'wɝθ'hwaɪl〕 *adj.* 值得的

This is a *worthwhile* book that deserves
your attention. (86 交大)

副 詞

absolutely 〔'æbsə,lutlɪ 〕 *adv.* 絕對地

He is *absolutely* the best basketball player
I have ever seen. (86 中興)

approximately 〔 ə'prɑksəmɪtlɪ 〕 *adv.*
大約

The area of the vacant lot is *approximately*
300 square meters. (87 台大)

```
ap + proxim + ate + ly
 |     |        |     |
to +  near   + adj. + adv.
```

attentively 〔 ə'tɛntɪvlɪ 〕 *adv.* 專心地

Studying *attentively*, he didn't hear the door
bell. (83 東吳)

B b

barely 〔'bɛrlɪ 〕 *adv.* 幾乎不

The change in population distribution was *barely* noticeable. (87 台大，86 中原，85 交大)

C c

considerably 〔 kən'sɪdərəblɪ 〕 *adv.*
相當大地

Her looks have changed *considerably*; I can hardly recognize her. (87 中原，85 文化)

cordially 〔'kɔrdʒəlɪ 〕 *adv.* 熱誠地

The host and hostess *cordially* welcomed their foreign guests. (84 政大，83 文化)

cord	+ ial	+ ly
heart	+ adj.	+ adv.

·Check List·

(   ) 1. vacant   A. crude

(   ) 2. vague   B. empty

(   ) 3. vexed   C. definitely

(   ) 4. vigorous   D. significantly

(   ) 5. vulgar   E. valuable

(   ) 6. vulnerable   F. healthful

(   ) 7. wholesome   G. alertly

(   ) 8. wicked   H. indistinct

(   ) 9. worthwhile   I. warmly

(   ) 10. absolutely   J. annoyed

(   ) 11. approximately   K. evil ; bad

(   ) 12. attentively   L. scarcely

(   ) 13. barely   M. susceptible

(   ) 14. considerably   N. roughly

(   ) 15. cordially   O. energetic

Vocabulary Ratings

5–7 *Good*   8–11 *Very Good*   12–15 *Excellent*

·Synonyms·

1. vacant
= empty

2. vague
= indistinct
= unclear

3. vexed
= annoyed
= upset

4. vigorous
= energetic
= dynamic

5. vulgar
= crude
= rude

6. vulnerable
= susceptible
= weak

7. barely
= scarcely
= hardly

8. wholesome
= healthful

9. wicked
= evil

10. worthwhile
= valuable

11. absolutely
= definitely
= undeniably

12. approximately
= roughly
= about

13. attentively
= alertly

14. considerably
= significantly
= greatly

15. cordially
= warmly

E e

eagerly 〔ˈigəlɪ〕 *adv.* 熱切地

She accepted the invitation *eagerly*. (85 文化)

enormously 〔ɪˈnɔrməslɪ〕 *adv.* 大大地

As photographic techniques have become more sophisticated, the scope of their application has expanded *enormously*. (86 中原)

entirely 〔ɪnˈtaɪrlɪ〕 *adv.* 完全地

It is *entirely* your fault that such a thing happened. (86 輔大)

F f

frequently 〔ˈfrikwəntlɪ〕 *adv.* 經常地

The young man is fond of movies, and goes to the theater *frequently*. (85 淡江)

I i

indistinctly 〔͵ɪndɪˈstɪŋktlɪ 〕*adv.* 模糊地

The island can only be seen *indistinctly*
because of the fog. (86 政大)

individually 〔͵ɪndəˈvɪdʒʊəlɪ 〕*adv.* 個別地

The candies are wrapped *individually*, each
one in a different color of paper. (86 交大)

in	+ divid	+ ual	+ ly
not	+ *divide*	+ *adj.*	+ *adv.*

intentionally 〔 ɪnˈtɛnʃənḷɪ 〕*adv.* 故意地

The boy made the mistake *intentionally*. He
wanted to get his parents' attention. (85 清大)

ironically 〔 aɪˈrɑnɪkḷɪ 〕*adv.* 諷刺地

Ironically, the judge himself committed a
serious crime. (83 輔大)

M m

meekly 〔'miklɪ〕 *adv.* 溫馴地

The little girl *meekly* obeyed all the commands her master gave. (84 成大)

O o

occasionally 〔ə'keʒənl̩ɪ〕 *adv.* 偶爾

I like to smoke a cigar *occasionally*. (82 政大)

officially 〔ə'fɪʃəlɪ〕 *adv.* 正式地

Officially, he is the head of the company, but it is really his son that does all the work.

(86 中原)

P p

perpetually 〔pə'pɛtʃʊəlɪ〕 *adv.* 永遠地

Throughout most of their lives, human beings *perpetually* learn and increase their mental capacities. (82 淡江)

primarily 〔'praɪ,mɛrəlɪ 〕 *adv.* 主要地

The charity *primarily* helps the sick, but it also takes care of the homeless. (87 中興)

prim	+ ari	+ ly
first	+ *adj.*	+ *adv.*

R r

rarely 〔'rɛrlɪ 〕 *adv.* 很少

I *rarely* swim in the winter because it is too cold. (86 中原)

reasonably 〔'riznəblɪ 〕 *adv.* 合理地

Margaret bought the coat because it was *reasonably* priced. (88 政大，83 交大)

regularly 〔'rɛgjələ·lɪ 〕 *adv.* 定期地

We should have our teeth checked by a dentist *regularly*.

(84 私醫)

reg	+ ular	+ ly
rule	+ *adj.*	+ *adv.*

repeatedly〔rɪ'pitɪdlɪ〕*adv.* 一再地

He made the same mistake *repeatedly*.
Obviously he didn't pay attention.

（85 文化，82 交大）

re	+ peat	+ ed	+ ly
again	+ *seek*	+ *adj.*	+ *udv.*

respectfully〔rɪ'spɛktfəlɪ〕*adv.* 恭敬地

The men removed their hats *respectfully*
when the flags passed by.（82 成大）

respectively〔rɪ'spɛktɪvlɪ〕*adv.* 個別地

Tom and Dave are a doctor and a lawyer
respectively.（86 中興）

S s

scarcely〔'skɛrslɪ〕*adv.* 幾乎不

He left in such a hurry that I *scarcely* had
time to thank him.（85 台大）

skillfully 〔'skɪlfəlɪ〕 *adv.* 有技巧地

Using words *skillfully* means not only choosing the right words but saying the words with the right tone. (87 政大，86 中興)

somewhat 〔'sʌm,hwɑt〕 *adv.* 有點

I was *somewhat* disappointed when Joe said he wasn't coming with us. (82 交大，81 輔大)

sparsely 〔'spɑrslɪ〕 *adv.* 稀少地

The whole region was *sparsely* settled by people from the frontier.

(87 成大)

```
sparse  +  ly
  |         |
scatter  +  adv.
```

steadily 〔'stɛdəlɪ〕 *adv.* 不斷地

Work hard, and you will improve *steadily*.

(85 文化)

U u

unexpectedly 〔ˌʌnɪkˈspɛktɪd 〕

adv. 意外地

To our surprise, Mary showed up at the party *unexpectedly*. (88 政大，85 文化)

V v

virtually 〔ˈvɝtʃʊəlɪ 〕 *adv.* 幾乎

After the earthquake, the building was *virtually* in ruins. (87 中央)

vividly 〔ˈvɪvɪdlɪ 〕 *adv.* 生動地

He *vividly* described his expeditions to the American West in his journals.

(87 中央，84 交大、私醫)

```
viv  +  id  +  ly
 |       |     |
live  +  adj. + adv.
```

•Check List•

( ) 1. eagerly   A. sometimes

( ) 2. entirely   B. seldom

( ) 3. intentionally   C. thinly

( ) 4. ironically   D. habitually

( ) 5. occasionally   E. surprisingly

( ) 6. perpetually   F. keenly

( ) 7. primarily   G. practically

( ) 8. rarely   H. sarcastically

( ) 9. regularly   I. slightly

( ) 10. somewhat   J. mainly

( ) 11. sparsely   K. totally

( ) 12. steadily   L. repeatedly

( ) 13. unexpectedly   M. deliberately

( ) 14. virtually   N. lively

( ) 15. vividly   O. forever

Vocabulary Ratings

5–7 *Good*   8–11 *Very Good*   12–15 *Excellent*

·Synonyms·

1. eagerly
   = keenly

2. entirely
   = totally
   = completely

3. intentionally
   = deliberately
   = on purpose

4. steadily
   = repeatedly
   = constantly

5. occasionally
   = sometimes

6. perpetually
   = forever
   = permanently

7. primarily
   = mainly
   = chiefly

8. rarely
   = seldom

9. regularly
   = habitually

10. somewhat
    = slightly
    = kind of

11. ironically
    = sarcastically

12. sparsely
    = thinly

13. unexpectedly
    = surprisingly

14. virtually
    = practically
    = nearly
    = almost

15. vividly
    = lively

單字索引

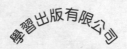

學習出版有限公司

單字口袋書系列

● 國 中 系 列

最基本1000字
劉　毅 主編
書售價120元 / 書+CD 售價380元

最基本1000字分類記憶
黃靜宜 主編
書售價150元 / 書+CD 售價390元

國中常用2000字
劉　毅 主編 / 書售價180元

國中分類記憶2000字
劉　毅 主編 / 書售價180元

升高中關鍵500字
劉　毅 主編 / 書售價180元

高中高職系列

高中常用7000字

劉 毅 主編 / 書售價220元

升大學成語1000

劉 毅 主編 / 書售價220元

升大學必考1000字

劉 毅 主編
書售價220元 / 書+CD 售價480元

進階字彙系列

四技二專1000字

周岳曇 主編 / 書售價220元

插大必考1000字

蔡琇瑩 主編
書售價220元 / 書+CD 售價480元

研究所必考1000字

林愔予 主編 / 書售價220元

心得筆記欄

心得筆記欄

心得筆記欄

Editorial Staff

- **主編** / 蔡琇瑩

- **校訂** / 謝靜芳・蔡文華・石支齊
  張碧紋・林銀姿・林愔子
  周岳曇・陳子璇・王　晴
  吳芸眞・劉　毅

- **校閱** / Laura E. Stewart

- **封面設計** / 白雪嬌

- **版面構成** / 黃淑貞

|||||||||||||● **學習出版公司門市部** ●|||||||||||||

台北地區：台北市許昌街 10 號 2 樓　TEL：(02)2331-4060‧2331-9209

台中地區：台中市綠川東街 32 號 8 樓 23 室　TEL：(04)2223-2838

|||||||||||||||||||||||||||||||||||||||||||||||||||||||||||||||||||||||||||||

插大必考 1000 字

主　　　編 / 蔡琇瑩

發　行　所 / 學習出版有限公司　☎ (02) 2704-5525

郵　撥　帳　號 / 0512727-2 學習出版社帳戶

登　記　證 / 局版台業 *2179* 號

印　刷　所 / 裕強彩色印刷有限公司

台 北 門 市 / 台北市許昌街 10 號 2 F

　　　　　　　☎ (02) 2331-4060‧2331-9209

台 中 門 市 / 台中市綠川東街 32 號 8 F 23 室 ☎ (04) 2223-2838

台灣總經銷 / 紅螞蟻圖書有限公司　☎ (02) 2795-3656

美國總經銷 / Evergreen Book Store　☎ (818) 2813622

本公司網址　www.learnbook.com.tw

電子郵件　learnbook@learnbook.com.tw

> 售價：新台幣二百二十元正

2004 年 4 月 1 日一版二刷